The Well

WHAT HAPPENS WHEN THE MIND RELEASES BUT THE HEART SUSTAINS?

Colleen Golden

outskirtspress

DENVER, COLORADO

Outskirts Press, Inc.
http://www.outskirtspress.com

ISBN: 978-1-4327-9943-4

Outskirts Press and the "OP" logo are trademarks belonging to Outskirts Press, Inc.

PRINTED IN THE UNITED STATES OF AMERICA

*To our grandparents, for all that they are,
and all that they bestow.*

Acknowledgments

Utmost appreciation goes to my husband, the consummate listener, cheering squad, and constructive critic, whose love and support soars above and beyond what I ever thought possible. Also, a heartfelt thanks to the Colorado Intrepid Ladies, to Shari, Bev, Annie, Elisa, Deb, Mary C. and other friends who patiently read the manuscript and offered suggestions and encouragement. Thank you to Rob, Dave, Aunt Betty, and other family members who helped resurrect old memories and factoids of life in the American Heartland, and to the surprisingly young writers who listened to excerpts and told me how much the story resonated with them and their own families. Lastly, thanks to my parents, who gave me the confidence to keep plodding even when there didn't seem to be an end in sight.

Prologue

I pull off my boots, check for the tattered prayer book reliably secured in my coat pocket, and climb up to balance on the edge of the well. My toes curl in protest to the icy rim of stone.

I feel renewed loathing at how the water's shimmering opacity seems to mock me.

Why doesn't this well have any reflection? It's just evil. I should at least be able to see the moon; it's full as a marshmallow.

My oldest son's voice echoes from below. "I'm sorry, Lily, it's the best thing for her and for us. You think I'm being a monster now, but you'll thank me after this is all over."

Then the cowboy's voice chimes in, again. "You can do it, Grace. You're The Baker. It's time."

More terrified than I've ever been in my life, I grab the rope with one hand, plug my nose with the other, shut my eyes, and step forward into the well.

Chapter 1

The Baker

I'm standing at the portal.

Again.

Not sure how I made my way back to it. Dang, but it is pretty! It dazzles like diamonds, but there's an eerie, pulsating glow from the other side. It lights up the snowflakes swirling around me, but I don't feel cold. In fact, I don't feel much of anything.

Been locked in a coma for a few months now. It's made me kind of confused, and more than a little cranky.

But please, no pity. My body is a wreck, but my mind, well, let's just say I've become a transcendental traveler. At least that's what my granddaughter, Iris, would say. I just adore her, but she's studying Psychology and she has some pretty strange ideas. She tried to tell me about something called "transaccidental medication," or something like that. From what I can tell, some people pay a lot of money to a guy wearing a towel on his head so's he'll give them a special word to say, over and over and over and over. She called it a "manta ray" or some other kind of fish. Supposed to make them feel spiritual, and maybe a bit nautical, I guess.

But maybe it's not so different from when I say the

rosary, or when those monks over in Tibet or India say their prayer wheels. At least that's what I read in Life magazine one time. Anyway, I had to laugh to myself because kids always think they've discovered or invented something that has actually been around for ages, only now it has a new name.

I did the same thing when I was young. Oh, I feel young enough now, even though my body is 76 years old.

I could aim my thoughts through this portal...but I recall last time I did, something happened that was very peculiar. Turned me into a scaredy little rabbit and I cottontailed it out of there. Now there's a big hole in my memory. I just hate when that happens. Do you have any people in your family with holes in their memory?

My name is Grace. My family is worried sick about me. I feel terrible and awful and sad about it, but there's not much I can do. So I try not to dwell on my problems. I don't want you to dwell on them, either. I am actually having a grand and fantastic adventure, but nobody can hear me, so I'm telling you about it here.

But first, I have to tell you some of the hard stuff. About how it all started. Mama told me, "get the hard part over with, then you can enjoy the good part." At the time I was going through a really long hard part, and I asked her, "what if the hard part never ends?"

"It will, though," she said, and she was right. It just took a while. So hang with me, and that's what we'll do.

THE WELL

I guess it was around my 75th birthday when my family started noticing odd little quirks in my behavior. They started teasing about my spells of "foggy dew." That just made me so mad.

Heck, I managed my Iowa farmstead and raised three children; what's the big deal if I drift off in the middle of a conversation? Maybe folks just aren't as interesting to me as they used to be, after all those years of listening to them jaw and yammer?

"Hey," I told them. "If you had as much on your mind as I do, you would be a lot worse than foggy."

But between you and me, even I was starting to wonder. Imagine my embarrassment when my neighbor, Doris Hansen, had to drive me home after I got lost on a county road I'd been traveling all my life. Then I started confusing my kids and grandkids with older relatives who had already given up the mortal coil, which is a fancy way of admitting that I started talking to ghosts. Uh-huh. I know what you're thinking.

Of course, in our little farm community, people carried out their lives in a natural rhythm, and senility was accepted as a part of normal aging. We just called it "Old-timers."

What no one realized until too late was that I had something different from normal aging. Inside my otherwise healthy head, a tiny little thing called a thyroid gland was winding down like an old clock. A simple enough problem to treat and manage, had my fool doctor diagnosed it.

But they left it untreated for months, which turned into

years. My condition deteriorated into heart disease, which in turn led to a run of small strokes that, over time, resulted in a slow decline of what folks used to call the "mental faculties." In other words, my brain started shutting down.

Gradually I lost my appetite for food and my interest in daily life. My own daughter, Lily, scolded me as if I were a child — can you imagine the nerve? — about the dust I allowed to gather on Grandma's antique mahogany chifferobe.

As if dust could hurt anyone. What is this, a white glove inspection?

My beloved garden, where I worked in the stifling humidity for years and harvested thousands of cans of tomatoes, green beans and peppers, was going to seed.

I even left my prize-winning honey beehives untended. One day, Lily found one hive depleted of its swarm, another with larvae both above and below the queen excluder, and the frames in the third overflowing with unharvested honey. I came upon her muttering angrily, "I need to get Chester over here to take care of these bees," as she picked up my bee veil and smoker from the pigsty where I had carelessly abandoned them.

I was outraged, and demanded to know, "Who left my stuff laying around like that? Must be Luke and Michael, where are those little boys? I'll tan their hides with the wooden spoon, soon as I catch them." Lily frowned at me, and I wondered, *Why is she looking at me so sad? I never really spank any of them.*

Folks I'd known all my life took to popping in unannounced, just like always, but they found me fussy and confused, still in my flannel nightgown, my hair in a disheveled heap around my face, babbling about a lost possession or a long dead pet.

They should have called ahead, isn't that the polite thing to do?

As they asked after my health, I fretted, *Now who in tarnation is this? Doesn't she know I'm busy, got a family to take care of here, need to get dinner started. Maybe some oatmeal. Are those kids up yet? They'll miss the school bus!*

After Hiram, my husband of fifty years, suddenly passed away, the kids became increasingly concerned for my safety. Eventually, my oldest son Luke found a nearby "senior residence." That's advertising talk for an old folks' depository, in case you don't know. He broke the news to Lily and my youngest, Michael, in my farmhouse kitchen. I could hear their voices, all hushed and serious, mingled with the drone of the TV.

Oh, they went on about how the place seemed nice, and the food was okay, and a bunch of other *la-dee-dah* that I really don't recall. I love all my kids the same, but I really was tired of their sibling disagreements. Lily and Luke were jealous of Michael, just like they'd been as youngsters when he saved up enough money to buy a brand new bicycle.

Luke had his future handed to him. The first son

inherited the farm; that's how it always worked. Lily also enjoyed a sweet deal as the elementary school's first grade teacher. How hard could that be? Could they really blame Michael for fleeing the farm country and making a life for himself where he wasn't surrounded by cornfields and cows? I recall lots of times I wanted to do the same, but never had the chance or the wherewithal.

It turned out that Michael was going to foot the bill, and return to New York. Lily and Luke promised to check in on me. But I didn't know much about any of that.

They could check in on me all they wanted; I was still checking out.

About a month later, when the big red oak trees in our farmyard blazed in the crisp autumn air, my family moved me into Sunset Suites. I immediately nicknamed it Beige Blather, because the cramped rooms were decorated in all neutrals – "Earth tones" they called it, as if Earth was ever that boring - and the residents seemed to be carrying on a muttering monologue to no one in particular. Blathering.

It was the second time I had moved in my whole life. The first time was when Hiram moved me, his 20-year-old bride, into the century-old white clapboard farmhouse, which would shelter us and ours for another half-century to come.

What are these kids up to now? What are they doing with my things?

I don't mean to whine. They did their best. But how do you squeeze an entire lifetime into a 10-foot square space? I swear, my root cellar was bigger.

They tucked undergarments and pajamas into the drawers under the vanity mirror, hung dresses in the niche that passed for a closet, and arranged toiletry items, a few of my favorite knickknacks, my reading glasses and my Bible on the nightstand within easy reach. My great granny's quilt hung over the edges of the twin bed, hiding the wicker basket of needlework stashed underneath it. A haloed, doe-eyed and serenely enraptured Jesus Christ gazed his blessing upon me from a water-stained picture hanging on the wall, just as he had done for Hiram and me all those fifty years.

For the umpteenth time, I considered drawing a moustache and derby hat on him with a black pen, and quickly asked God for forgiveness.

"What about her rocking chair?" Luke asked. I sat on the bed, preoccupied with Christ's imaginary makeover, vaguely registering the fact that they were talking about me as if I weren't there.

Lily sighed and smoothed back her hair. "There just isn't room, Luke. There's barely room to get around the bed."

"I feel like that chair is a part of her. She rocked all her babies in it, and did her sewing and reading there while Dad did paperwork on the kitchen table."

"I know. I feel terrible about it. I feel terrible about

all of it. I just hope that getting good care will help her to improve, at least a little bit. Meanwhile, I guess she's traded her rocking chair for a wheelchair." She shook her head. "Sorry, I didn't intend that to sound like a bad joke."

I chuckled, though. Chair for chair. Lily could be kind of witty sometimes. Probably got that from Hiram. He was a man of few words, but what he said was usually well thought out, and he could come up with little zingers when you least expected it. He was a good man, and I do miss him, although I had to ply him with liquor to get him to dance with me.

Sure enough, she found that wheelchair in the hallway and helped me into it. I felt cranky and tried to squirm out of it, demanding to go home. She feigned cheerfulness, but I could hear her stomach rumbling like an old tractor.

"Sit tight, Mother, and I'll take you on a tour. You see? It's a nice place; they keep it real clean and pretty. They just painted all the walls this nice sand color. Here's the dining room, and over there is the common area for watching television and all, and look, out there is the patio garden."

"Why are you talking like such a ninny?" I grumped at her. "I can see for myself what they have, and I want to go home."

"Mom, please just keep an open mind. We'll come see you every day. Just give it a try, OK?"

What a lot of hooey!

Hadn't I survived more than she could ever imagine? I'd

been witness to a whole host of world events, which tumbled and cascaded like the dominoes my kids set up on the old wooden table where we shared thousands of meals. The strange thing was that even though I couldn't tell you what I ate for lunch, I could remember those long ago things just fine: Four ghastly wars and the bloody carnage of far-off places with names like Passchendaele, Normandy and Hiroshima; tearing out our walls to put in indoor plumbing (Praise God!); the Flappers and all their folderol; pinching pennies and eating beans for weeks all through the Great Depression; the furious debates over President Roosevelt's New Deal.

We could escape a lot of it for a few hours of Hollywood's silver-screen glitz on Saturday matinees. Then we tore up the walls again for our wondrous new electrical wiring, then came telephones – first the party line (so everybody knew everybody else's business), then private lines all to ourselves. Next came newfangled appliances, like my wringer washing machine and electric mixer, radios and television, black & white at first, then in full color like that network's peacock tail!

Not to mention the highway network that spider-webbed across the country's vast prairies and deserts and mountains to free up the automobiles streaming out of Detroit like the endless stream of red ants from the giant anthill behind our barn.

How astonished we were when the Wright boys flew

their newfangled machines! Of course, now there's those jet airplanes. Rockets to outer space, even! Bless me.

They erected the world's tallest building in New York City (I always kind of thought it reflected some men's wishful thinking. *I mean, really, who wants their feet to be that far off the ground?*). Then there was the rise and eventual fall of Prohibition *(more folderol),* and the New York World's Fair *(I'm still steamed that I didn't get to go).*

Who is she, this uppity daughter of mine, to tell me how things are?

Through all the days of my life, I wove those worldly affairs into my own tapestry of childhood, marriage, and the lives of my children and grandchildren. A tapestry whose warp and woof consisted of my garden and honey beehives, savory pots of chicken and dumplings, endless cakes, pies, biscuits and gravy, towers of washed dishes, mountains of washing to hang on the line, summers when we prayed for rain and winters when we prayed for sun, stuffy church services followed by gossipy potlucks, the Sunday school classes I taught and 4H projects I mentored.

The seasons of lack or plenty punctuated by bone numbing, never ending work. Yes, I could tell my daughter a thing or two.

But in the end, I didn't really feel like arguing with Lily. Even though I only completed my schooling through sixth grade, it's always been up to me to hold a steady course in life, so that those around me can jostle and sway without losing their bearings. This just seemed like another one of those times.

Shoot! Here I am talking about a steady course while I'm meandering.

Back to this portal. The light seems to be winking at me, teasing, beckoning, and the strangest of all...I swear I can hear my mother's voice singing on the other side of it. She's long dead, of course. There's a ticklish recollection of baking. Maybe I baked something there?

That would make some sense. You see, even though I was kind of a "looker" in my day, with Mama's shiny, dark hair and mint green eyes, there wasn't room in my farm budget for a woman's vanities. So I developed my name and fame as a baker. My velvety cakes and lattice top pies were always big hits at the State Fair. Folks said that I could take a batch of dough and "turn it into a little slice of Heaven!"

But after the kids moved me into Beige Blather, I realized my baking days were over.

I became increasingly oblivious to the nursing home's bustle. My "foggy dew" slowly expanded into an enfolding landscape that blanketed my mind in softly falling snow, muffling the rest of my existence. Memories alighted like snowflakes on a child's mitten, only to melt away just as I thought I recognized them. Showers, meals and other mundane activities began to come as surprises to me, moments of color popping up without warning in the snowdrifts.

I continued slipping away until the winter of 1984,

when my family agreed to have a gastronomy tube placed into my stomach. That means I was getting food and water through that tube! What a jip!

Then they started carrying on with all kinds of foolishness, trying to get a response from me.

The portal lights are brighter now, humming with a steady gleam, and I swear that is Mama's voice I'm hearing, singing an old church hymn. Yes, that's it. "In the Sweet By and By..."

⚜

"I swear, Iris, we've gone way over the top trying to wake Mama up. We've done read-alouds, held one-sided conversations where we keep talking even though she doesn't answer, tried mild tickling, then we started in with music. You know how she loved music and dancing. Oh, your grandmother was a beauty in her day!

"She had gorgeous legs, and she would jitterbug around the kitchen until a waltz came on the radio, then Daddy would grab hold and lead her around like they were Fred and Ginger. They looked so happy then.

"Anyway, we tried all kinds of music. First the old gospel and country favorites, then Glenn Miller, Andrews Sisters, you know, the Lawrence Welky stuff, then we tried John Philip Sousa, bagpipe bands, Slavonic Dances, even some hip-hop blasted through the room. I think the other residents actually like it, but we did tax the patience of the nursing staff.

"Then we put on some comedy skits and fake melo-dramas complete with costumes and props, sprayed the air with the jasmine and citrus aromatherapy, and even projected a laser light show onto the walls of her room."

"And she didn't show any sign she heard or saw you?" Iris, Lily's daughter, looked up from her embroidery.

"Oh, every now and then, she twitched an eyelid or murmured 'hmm' aloud before clamming up again. We thought maybe that meant she was slowly coming around. After all, wasn't she always going on at us about the importance of not giving up?" Lily turned away and stared out the window.

The truth was that as the days, weeks, and then months passed, the family started to give up, slowly withdrawing from Grace, first into their own silences, then a full retreat into their own lives. No one wanted to verbalize what seemed obvious: Grace was locked in.

Iris put down her needlework and regarded her mother. She was studying Psychology, for God's sake. There must be something she could say to ease her mother's mind and cheer herself up. "What if Grandma has taken her mind to someplace better than here?"

"What do you mean?"

"I mean maybe she isn't really 'here' in the conventional way anymore. No one knows what happens to people when they're in comas, you know? Seriously, how long has it been since she opened her eyes and spoke to anyone?"

Out of habit, Lily glanced at the garden calendar on the wall. "Six months now." Her voice wavered. "I would never admit this to your Uncle Luke or Uncle Michael, but I'm starting to forget what her voice sounds like." She swallowed hard. "At first I was sure that she would come out of it. So sure that I literally waited here, day in, day out, almost afraid to breathe sometimes for fear I might miss a little sign that she was coming back to life. It was easier to hope when people were coming and doing all their silliness." She gave a half smile. "Made it seem like this was all just a bad dream and soon Mom and the rest of us would all wake up."

Lily pulled a flowered handkerchief out of her purse and Iris caught a whiff of her mother's favorite Chantilly perfume. Lily rubbed her temples, grimacing with a headache. "And Michael, he's miles away, not just distance miles, but person miles, you know? Sometimes I can't even think of him as my baby brother who used to take off running buck naked down the dirt road, laughing and screaming to wake the dead with Mom chasing after him. Now it's like he's family, but more of a distant cousin than a brother. He wheels up in that little, red sports car and out steps this guy from a slick magazine ad, in his white linen shirt and pressed khakis and tasseled Italian loafers. Shoot! I hardly recognize him."

Iris found a Tylenol package in her backpack and handed

it to Lily. "Be fair, Mom. He's worked hard, and he's successful. And that's how we can afford to give Grandma such good care, right? No matter where he lives, she's still his mom, I know he loves her."

"I just can't help but feel like he's a little embarrassed by his hick family, and he's already written Mom off."

"Maybe he's dealing the only way he knows how. What else can he do? He lives a thousand miles away! He's doing his part by paying for the nursing home. You told me that was the agreement, everyone is doing their part, and together you're all doing what's best for Grandma."

Lily sighed. "I know, honey, I'm just tired and discouraged. It's getting harder and harder to keep my hopes up. But then I read about these cases where people are in comas for years, until suddenly, one day, for no reason that anyone understands, they come back. So then I think how terrible it would be to give up too soon, and miss the chance to have her back.

"It's easier in the daytime. With the sun up I can imagine her coming back to life. But at night, in bed, after your father's gone to sleep, I just lay awake studying the darkness. And I get so scared, Iris, that this is what her life will be like from now on, and that we are torturing her to not let her die."

"She doesn't seem to be in pain, more like in limbo. Maybe she's gone somewhere else… in her mind, I mean." Iris tried to look confident. "Maybe she's escaped to some wonderful dimension, and her body doesn't know it yet."

"Can't say that I buy into all that nonsense, Iris. At any rate, I can't give up on her." Lily turned away to hide her tears.

***

Yes, there is no mistaking Mama's sweet soprano. She's sounding nearer now. I can make out the words of her favorite old hymn, "There's a land that is fairer than day, and by faith we can see it afar." I join in, "In the sweet bye and bye," and move forward out of the snow, toward the glowing light, the warmth, the comfort…

Chapter 2

Let the Marvels Begin

Like a clarion bell, the voice continues, "In the sweet by and by, we shall meet on that beautiful shore." We sing the next few bars together.

I'm smiling as I shade my eyes against the brightness. *What is the next verse? Oh, yes. Something about, "and our spirit shall sorrow no more. Not a sigh for the blessing of rest."* A life-like memory of my mother flashes onto my mind's eye. It's one of those sultry summer afternoons when the very air seems to drip, and she stops taking clothes off the line for a moment to wipe the sweat from her eyes and glance over at me. The sun's brilliance silhouettes her against the horizon, and bedazzles the grass into a field of emeralds.

Am I dead, Mama? She laughs, then holds out her hand.

What would you do in my situation? Even though in some corner of my mind I know she's dead, I reach out and take her hand, floating along blindly through the sunlight, through the memory, all the way through the portal, and onward into … my own brightly lit kitchen, where I spent the better part of my better days.

I gaze around the room with my jaw dropped to the floor.

"Well, that's unexpected, seeing as how I thought maybe this might be Heaven or something. But I guess now I know I'm just dreaming, and not dead," I announce, a little surprised to hear my own voice.

The warm aromas of yeast, wheat and butter tease my nose. I run my hand over the cool aqua tile countertop with dingy grout that stubbornly resisted my lifelong efforts to keep it white, and skate-slide my shoes along the speckled linoleum floor, just as I used to play "skating" to trick the kids into mopping it.

"Let's find out how realistic this dream kitchen is." I pull out the bins my husband made to hold the large volumes of flour, sugar and cornmeal we used on a daily basis, feeding all those kids and farm hands, too. Sure enough, filled to the brim.

I jump when the radio on top of my Frigidaire crackles and comes alive with the voice of Minnie Pearl, queen of the forever $1.98 hat, loudly declaring how proud she is to be here. My white, dotted Swiss curtains that I bought up in Springfield are dancing in the breeze.

Despite my disappointment at not being in the Heavenly Kingdom, at least this is something familiar. Well, almost familiar. I look out the window, expecting to see the old barn and oak tree and my vegetable garden, and Hiram's tractor and the kids' bicycles. But instead there's just an amber mist surrounding the house.

I shrug off a vague uneasiness. *Dreams are always strange,*

*and besides, maybe there won't be so much work to do as there was
on the real farm.*

I sit down at the heavy oak table, then look around and
realize that every surface, the table, the counters, the tops
of the bread bin and toaster, all of it is covered with blobs
of dough. Bread dough, noodle dough, pie dough, even
doughnuts waiting to be deep-fried. Sakes Alive! All this
dough! I laugh out loud for the joy of it.

Now, mind you, I baked nearly every day for fifty years.
I know, as all bakers know, that dough, despite its simplicity,
presents an endless array of possibilities. And this kitchen
seems to have an infinite supply of it.

"Well, this could be downright ducky." I grab my red-
checkered apron off the hook on the wall, and tie it around
my waist.

In Grace's room at Sunset Suites, Iris tried to reassure
her mother. "Mom, you're doing all you can for her, and
you're right, sometimes people *do* wake up from these per-
sistent vegetative states, and it *is* too soon to know. Doctors
have been wrong before! Miracles happen every day, right?
You tell me about them all the time."

Lily touched the wadded handkerchief to her tongue
and wiped wet makeup streaks from her face.

"Oh, those are just things I read in the tabloids, I don't
know if they're really true. It's just so creepy trying to go

on with a normal life. I get up and make breakfast, just like normal, I go to work and teach my kids, just like normal, then I come here, and there's this little mannequin who looks like my mother, but it can't possibly be my mother because my mother could run circles around all of us, and I talk and read to this mannequin who of course says nothing, and I think maybe I'm going crazy! Something is very wrong with the world!"

Lily crumpled in her chair and began to sob. Iris reached over and stroked her hair, until she calmed and pulled away.

"All I really hope is that somehow, some way, Mother is aware of everything we're doing for her, hoping for her, praying for her."

Iris choked back her own tears and decided to resort to religion. That was Grandma's mainstay, maybe it would help Lily. "Maybe she's in some kind of Purgatory. Maybe she's getting that over with now, as a prelude to making her way to Heaven. Isn't that what she believed?"

Lily glanced up with a wry smile. "Purgatory, huh? I don't know if that happens before you actually die. But if that's the case, at least she doesn't have to be alone while she goes through it. Either Luke or I or one of your cousins come every day and talk and read to her, just in case she can hear us."

That was it. "Say! How about if I start writing letters to her about graduate school and Poppy and everything, that would give you something else to read to her, and make me feel like at least I haven't abandoned her."

Lily pulled her close again. "That's my sweet girl. What a wonderful idea! And even if Mother can't hear you, I will enjoy those letters myself! It will make me feel like I'm seeing you and my only grandbaby even though you're so far away, up in Detroit."

Meanwhile, just down the hall, a staff nurse named Jessica sighed as she helped a frail, elderly woman into the white tiled shower. These double shifts were so exhausting, she wasn't sure it was worth the extra money. But at least Ernestine was alert and chatty. Looking like a garden gnome in her shower cap with ears sticking out, she smiled at Jessica and tittered, "I have a boyfriend."

Jessica adjusted the water temperature and began sponging her, smiling in amusement. "You do? That's great!"

Her patient squirmed with the delight of sharing a secret. "And he's young and handsome, and he visits me late at night, and we make whoopee!" She waved both hands in front of her like windshield wipers, rolling her eyes with a naughty giggle.

Jessica clucked her tongue. "Gee, I wish I had a young, handsome boyfriend like that!" she teased. *Poor thing, her thoughts are knit looser than my old sweater. But hey, at least she's enjoying herself, and who woulda' thought?* She finished drying Ernestine and tucked her in. "Now sleep tight, and don't wear out that boyfriend of yours, you brazen hussy!" They both laughed as she turned out the light and left the room.

A few weeks later, Jessica was just starting her usual night shift when she overheard one of the more lucid patients yelling loudly at the front desk clerk: "I'm telling you, I want another room! There's a pervert coming into my room at night!" The clerk was stammering incoherently.

With a cold feeling in her stomach, Jessica approached them. "I'll handle this, Tina. Now what's going on, Ms. Sager?" She leapt out of the way just in time to avoid having her foot run over by the woman's wheelchair.

"You people don't have a clue, do you? There is a man coming into the rooms at night! Doesn't anyone supervise here? You need a security guard! And I want a new room, with a deadbolt lock on the door!"

"We'll move you right now to a room closer to the nurse's station, no problem," Jessica patted her shoulder and turned her chair around. "And don't worry, I'll be looking into this." Her earlier conversation with Ernestine percolated into awareness.

I open up the bins in my imaginary kitchen and rub my hands together. "At least this dream will be more interesting than nothing but fog and snow. I might as well bake something."

I begin cutting hunks of butter into bowls full of flour and herbs or spices. I add bubbly yeast water, knead, wait, and take up a hunk of the warm, pliant stuff to see how it molds. I start with old favorites at first: flaky biscuits, gooey cinnamon buns, dense loaves of crusty bread, noodle puddings. It seems that as I bake, my memory improves, and I can recall more and more recipes. I'm not sure how much time is passing, but there does seem to be some sort of change in the light - sunset and sunrise? - in this dream, so maybe days are drifting by.

Who cares? It's not like I'm on a timetable.

Eventually, as I wait for a rhubarb pie to bake, I am singing along to an old favorite on the radio: "Hot Diggity, Dog Ziggity, dum-dee-dum something something"...you know the one. As I sing, I absentmindedly shape some dough into a blob that vaguely resembles one of those little hot dog-shaped puppies.

Now I know this next part will sound pretty bonkers. Remember, I'm just telling you about my dream, right? Well, as I'm doughing and singing, the blob takes on form and color. Next thing I know, that dadburned puppy shape starts to tremble and shakes its doughy little tail.

When the little dachshund finally looks up at me and barks, I am so startled that I leap backwards, overturn my chair and land painfully on my rump. In a panic, I whisk my thoughts back through the gleaming archway of the portal, into the snow, and soon lose my way.

After bumbling around for a while, I hear Mother's voice again, and follow it back to the glow in the snow. My associations with it are pleasant enough, but I feel a little wary. Still, it's just so sweet-sounding, and the lights are so warm and welcoming. I slowly ease my thoughts back through the portal and into the kitchen, where everything is sure enough just as I left it, the chair overturned, a mess of dough on the floor, and a dachshund puppy at the screen door, whining to be let outside.

I open the door, watch him streak through the amber mist to God knows where, and sit down at my table. I fiddle with some dough, resurrecting the memory of my previous visit by talking it through.

"Huh. The weird thing about this dream is that I'm sitting here thinking and talking to myself, and I feel so awake. But it's got to be a dream, because my dough became a dog. Maybe I'll try something else, to test it out. Might as well make something I can use."

So I decide to bake a car. A loopy notion, I know. But I was so envious as a young woman when my snooty neighbor drove over in her shiny 1930 Packard Phaeton, orange with black doors. Out she stepped, all hotsy-totsy, looking like she was the Queen of England or something. Man! I really coveted that car.

Why not? Why not bake a car? This is my dream, after all.

So I imagine that car in my mind's eye, and shape a wad of dough that vaguely resembles it. I place the car blob on the table and sit back to watch as the dough … does nothing. I laugh at the absurdity of it. *What is wrong with me? A lump of dough is a lump of dough, no more, no less.*

I jump at the sound of barking and pawing at the screen door. *Good grief! I forgot about the puppy. He was just a lump of dough, and he sure seems real enough now.* I open the door and cradle the puppy while he licks my face clean with exuberant kisses.

"Now why is that?" I tease him. "Why did you come to life, and the car is still just a blob of dough?"

Aloud, I retrace my steps. "I shaped the dough, I didn't bake it, I just set it on the table and it became you." The dog cocks his head to one side and whines. "Wait a second, I remember now! I was singing a song about a hot dog, and there you were."

The dog barks excitedly. I set him down and search my memory for a song about a car. What was that old tune from the 1920's? *Oh yes ... I remember.* I start whistling and the words return to me: "I'm just wild about horns on cars and such that go..." and I whistle the tune.

As I continue singing, I stare, transfixed, while the dough solidifies, grows, and assumes the form and color of a full-size vintage automobile parked in my kitchen. The puppy and I regard it in stunned silence.

"Huh. Maybe I'd best continue this outdoors. Meanwhile, you, my friend, need a name. How about "Eureka?" I learned it back in our little schoolhouse; it means something like a surprise discovery. After all, you did make a pretty impressive entrance.

"So, Eureka, how often do I have a dream where I can

bake life size things? Time for some fun."

The next thing I "sculpt-sing" (because it's high summer in Iowa and the heat is suffocating) is a majestic oak tree that shaded my yard back home. For the first time in what seems like ages, I am really enjoying myself!

But you know every rose has thorns; a little twinge of doubt tickles my conscience.

"Am I trespassing on God's private property?" Eureka tilts his head, as if deliberating. "Is it really OK to be baking things that are alive, like, you know, you?"

He yawns lazily and plops on my feet.

"Oh, malarkey, it's just a puppy and a car and a tree. Where's the harm?"

But it *is* all pretty unnerving. In my experience, dough doesn't change into things like puppies, cars and trees.

It just violates all the basic rules of baking.

The puppy looks up at me, tongue flapping out one side of his mouth, eyes bright with expectation.

"Of course, you're right," I shake my head, smiling. "It's just a dang dream."

Chapter 3
Possibilities

1985

Mama used to say that when you're young, the days fly by, but a year is an eternity; and when you're old, the years fly by, but the days pass like slow molasses stuck in the jar.

I can tell you from personal experience that when you're in the nursing home, and your thoughts have become white snow, time doesn't go fast or slow. Time just doesn't exist. There's now, and now, and more now, until you're so sick of "now," you'd give your right arm for a "then," or a "soon" or even a "never."

But oddly enough, I'm not really bored, more like in suspended animation. I am aware that my loved ones continue to visit, and that is a genuine comfort for me and for them, too, I guess.

I hope.

❧❦❧

"I spoke with Aurora last night, Mom. She's your grand niece, remember?"

Lily flipped the calendar on Grace's wall to the new month. "She's driving down from Nebraska to visit for a few days. It's a long drive, but she left early and should be here any time now."

Lily noticed the new black and blue mottles on Grace's arms, the result of failed attempts at blood draws for the lab. She lifted the bedspread and placed it over Grace's arms, covering the bruises and leaving just her hands showing out the sides. She checked the chart hanging from the bedrail to see when the nurse would be coming in to change Grace's diaper and turn her body to a slightly different position. Without those frequent adjustments, she would develop painful and possibly dangerous bedsores on the pressure points where her skin touched the sheets without relief.

"Good," she mumbled aloud, "they just did her diaper and the turning. But I wish they would have given her the Ensure already, and she's due for a sponge bath, too."

Sponge baths were generally given every other day. Even though she wasn't perspiring, Grace's body exuded a mildly acrid scent of medication and wastes.

Lily pulled a cotton swab out of the package on the nightstand and applied some Vaseline to Grace's lips, which were dry and cracked. Her breath smelled stale and slightly decayed. They were supposed to send in the dentist to check her teeth.

"I need to ask the nurse about your dentist, Mom," Lily sighed as Grace remained still and quiet. "Just like you used to say, 'Life can be good, but it ain't perfect.' I can't believe your hair hasn't gone all grey. How the heck do you manage that?"

Lily gathered up the detritus of packaging and tissues that had collected on Grace's nightstand over the past day. "Don't now why they can't seem to throw things into the trash can," she muttered.

Then she checked her own reflection, mentally clucking at her own grey roots showing beneath the auburn tint, and the lines around her eyes. They seemed deeper. Some of the beads on her best white cardigan were hanging by loose threads. "Yep, that's pretty much how I feel these days, hanging by a loose thread."

Just then, Lily could hear Aurora making her way down the hall, exchanging pleasantries with the nurse. Her soft, hushed footsteps slowed as she eased her way through the door, a vase of flowers in one hand and a large shopping bag in the other. A large purse had slipped off her shoulder and dangled awkwardly from the crook of her elbow.

Lily laughed. "I would recognize that pack mule look anywhere! You must be a teacher." She took the vase and sniffed the flowers. "Mmm, I just love carnations."

She set it on the nightstand while Aurora put down everything else, and they hugged.

Aurora regarded Grace's silent form, then leaned over and spoke softly. "It's me, Auntie Grace, Aurora. Your sister and Abel's granddaughter, remember? You used to braid my doll's hair at our family picnics on the porch of the Shack, behind Grandpa Abel's amusement park."

She waited and watched for some sign of response, then turned to Lily, distressed. "How could this have happened to Aunt Grace? She was always so full of energy and life!"

The door banged open. "Good afternoon," a heavy-set nurse boomed. "Sorry, but I need to give her the Ensure now."

"That's fine," Lily replied. "We can just go get some coffee and come back in a few minutes." She doubted that Aurora had seen a gastronomy tube, and wanted to preserve as much of Grace's dignity as she could, even though it seemed to become an increasingly moot point every day.

They sat down at a round, grey formica table in the deserted cafeteria with styrofoam cups of bitter coffee from the vending machine. Aurora's dark eyes were troubled. "Are the nurses here always that abrupt?"

Agitated, Lily swallowed the coffee too quickly and winced as it burned her throat. "Some of the nurses are ex-military," she explained. "They are efficient in terms of doing things on schedule, but their bedside manner can leave a lot to be desired. I like the head nurse, Jessica, but she's off today."

She refrained from sharing Luke's cynical comments about the staff at Sunset Suites. ("I'm surprised they can get qualified people to work there at all, with the low wages they pay.")

"Lily, what exactly is going on with her? Is she going to get better?"

"I don't know if she is, honey, I keep praying and hoping, but no one seems to know for sure. People wear down. It's not like we have bodies that were meant to last forever, you know." She laughed softly. "Iris thinks that Mom's mind has gone somewhere else, someplace better. Or maybe to Purgatory. I don't know what to think about that."

Aurora shook her head and looked doubtful. "It's too bizarre to see her mute and still. I wonder if she can understand what's being said to her. She used to be the best listener, Lily. When I was little, I wondered if she could hear my thoughts, she was so good at knowing how I felt, or what I needed."

Lily smiled and nodded. "The times I tried to pull something over on her, she just tilted her head and squinted her eyes, like she was reading my mind! I used to kid her about being too dang spooky."

They both laughed at the memory, then went quiet.

"But do you think she knows what's happening to her? Do you think she feels any pain? It would kill me to think of her in pain." Aurora's eyes filled with tears.

Lily gazed out the window at endless rows of corn reaching toward the horizon. "I wish I knew. I wish I had some power or ability beyond what I have, so I could make this nightmare stop. I've enlisted the prayer circle at church, and even called up the evangelist TV show hotlines. Of course, those people always want you to drain your savings, as if you could purchase the Almighty's blessing with the almighty dollar.

"I confess to my own bargaining, though. I've made deals with God that if she could only get well, I'll stop doing this, or start doing that. I don't know what else to do, but to be here for her, and I can't be here all the time."

Lily's voice broke. Aurora reached for her hand. "I'm so sorry, Aunt Lily, I'm so, so sorry."

Lily shook her head as if coming up for air. "Sweetie, you've driven seven long hours and I'm not going to spend your time wallowing in self-pity." She squeezed Aurora's hand. "I'll be OK. You should go talk to Mom. I know you feel a little silly talking to a woman who doesn't move, but like you said, she was always a good listener! I have no idea if she can hear us or not, but I know she loves you, and she would want to hear your voice."

Once they returned to Grace's room, Aurora sat next to her and held up her photographs again. "Here's my family, Auntie Grace. They are so wonderful! I wish you could meet them."

Her voice wavered as she looked to Lily, who nodded and smiled in reassurance. "It helps if you pretend that she's answering you, and just keep talking."

Aurora inhaled deeply, straightening her shoulders. She began a monologue about the family picnics on the front porch of The Shack, under the shady canopy of oak trees behind the amusement park. "That was when Grandpa Abel was alive, of course," she added, and fought back tears again. "He was my hero, you know."

✥

Wherever or whatever this dream is, I am having a rollicking good time.

Feeling zesty about my new puppy, and car, and tree, I take some dough outside, shape up my honeybee hives, and sing some busy bees into them with Arthur Askey's old song. Corny tune, I know, but the only other one I recall is "A Bee in Your Boudoir." Sounds inadvisable, considering I already have a Phaeton in the kitchen.

Glorious sound and sight, all those black & yellow, industrious, humming little scoots!

"I've really missed you guys!"

Then on to the dry ditch in my front yard, where I sing a few bars from that song about Cripple Creek, and start the creek gurgling past the trees. Still singing, I set a covered bridge over the creek, complete with red paint, and, feeling ambitious, extend it with a newly paved road.

"This is much better than hanging out in the snowy acres of oblivion," I tell Eureka, who barks what sounds like agreement.

My previously "foggy" ideas are taking shape like soldiers on a battlefield. I have intentions! Ideas! Plans!

I pack a satchel with pouches of dough, add a sandwich, a thermos and some dog biscuits, call out to Eureka to come along, cross my new bridge over my new creek, and set out on my new road. Along the way I'm belting out the one about the red robin and populating my surroundings with songbirds. Their chirps and lilts set the perfect tone for a day of making up stuff. And it just keeps getting better.

As I move from song to song, the amber mist recedes, and my thoughts become more clear and confident. I figure it's time to get a little creative. Why not improve on the world as I knew it? *Who cares what I do in my dream?*

So I sculpt-sing a river fed by the creek, followed by some scattered farmhouses with tire swings hanging from grand shade trees and bright red barns, chicken coops, horse corrals, pigs in their pens and cows out to pasture. I add fields with plush rows of green corn and golden wheat, a tall granary and silo next to the Grange meeting hall (that's a little bittersweet, seeing it so empty), a railroad track bordering a county road, passing by a white clapboard school house and steepled church, a lumber mill and a Granny Smith apple orchard.

You know how everything gets easier with practice? I start making up songs of my own and belt out the melodies to the blue sky overhead, feeling all Aces.

Oh, wow, here's that pretty little meadow where I always thought a town should be. Why not?

I start with a Main Street lined with weeping willow and maple trees, a courthouse, bank, hotel and Sheriff's office, then a row of cottages with gardens and American flags on the porches, a corner grocery selling local produce and Archie and Katie Keene comic books for a nickel, a park with a big lake topped with water lilies, and a Library whose cool, columned entryway beckons.

Too good to be true, right? Can you blame me? Almost eighty years of places that lacked the niceties or even necessities, not to mention people who were either dumbbells or just plain mean. Think about it: if you had your chance to create a world, what would you put in it or leave out?

To set it all off, I add an ice cream truck broadcasting calliope music.

Let's face it, we could all use a little ice cream.

All along the way, I place trees. *Let's see, I like maples, oaks, and fruit trees, oh, and some evergreens for the winter. "Oh Tannenbaum." Need more birds. Wrens, terns, bluebirds, cardinals, owls, woodpeckers, goldfinches, hummingbirds, whip-poor-wills, killdeers, pheasants, peacocks. Oh, and butterflies, too.* My hands are flying, my voice ringing out like a bell, bits of dough spinning off all around me, taking shape almost as quickly as I can call forth the thoughts.

"Yippee and Jubilation!"

Time for the Town Center. I'm going full bore now!

"Let's see... what all did I see back in Springfield?"

A few privately owned dress and curio shops; a five-and-dime with sparkly costume jewelry and perfumes from Paris; and a shiny, red soda fountain counter with black leather stools housed in the art deco Kresge building where skinny mannequins posed in the window wearing high fashion.

"Never knew I was such a world-class sculptor!" I holler to Eureka, who yaps happily from my satchel, his legs too tired to keep up on foot.

I add more business offices downtown, a mill and factory closer to the train track and river, and a small airstrip on the outskirts.

Who knows when I might feel like taking a flight? First one, ever!

Then I start recalling scenes from the picture shows. A designer boutique, a grand old hotel appointed with the finest marble and brass fancywork, a sidewalk cafe with bright green and white awnings, and – Ta Da! - a country club with tennis courts and a marina fronting the lake.

Hey, I may live on a farm and only got through sixth grade, but I'm no dummy.

OK, speaking of school, that's enough tomfoolery. I get serious and mold a brick and ivy university, a modern hospital, and a prison, all within the town limits, based on my ever more vivid recollections.

Assuming my best imitation of Jackie Gleason on The Honeymooners, I declare, "With dough like this, who needs money?" and laugh out loud.

At last, I step back to admire my handiwork. "Hmm, look at that! My little place has become a town."

I reflect that every town needs a name.

"Possibilities! Yes, that's it. In honor of my magical kitchen and its versatile dough." I am deeply and refreshingly satisfied.

Whew, it is hot out! I return to my farm, squeeze some lemons for lemonade, plop a straw into my favorite green rubberized glass, grab my sunhat and walk barefoot to the hammock, squishing the cool grass between my toes.

Stretched out in the netting between two trees and looking forward to a leisurely nap, I am surprised to hear a muffled but familiar voice. I sit up, hopeful.

Maybe there will be some other people in this dream. I could use some company.

I cock my ear toward the sound, starting to make out isolated words here and there. I stand, look around, and follow the voice toward the barn. As I round the corner of the old red building, I am amazed to find the wooden arch, sideposts and stone walls of an old well.

What the ... ? Where did this come from? We never had a well.

I lean over and stare down at water that shines and glistens with silvery light.

But something is very wrong.

Where is my reflection? Am I invisible? Oh, well, maybe just a trick of the light. But I think that voice is coming from here.

I listen carefully. Sure enough, the voice is echoing from somewhere in the water ... or maybe underneath the water. I can't be positive.

I shouldn't be surprised. Anything can happen in dreams. After all, I've just spent the morning putting up a new town; how weird is that? So now it seems that there are people living under well water.

I brace my hands on the mossy stone of the well, and lean in toward the water.

The voice continues, a little warbly. "He was my hero, you know. Even though it's been eight years since he died, I still feel like he's around. Grandpa Abel was such a force in the world."

No way! She's talking about my sister's husband, Abel MacGregor. What's that about him being gone? Impossible. That old hellion? He's out there raising Cane somewhere — ha! I'm punny.

A tug at the sleeve of my memory. There had been something about Abel, way back before I started feeling foggy in my mind. Something about his funeral, and how they didn't think I should go. Or did I go? It was all so confusing.

But if you never heard of Abel McGregor, let me tell you, he was indeed a "force in the world."

Chapter 4

The Hero and the Yellow Carousel Horse

Aurora turned to Lily and spoke more quietly, "There's something else about Grandpa I wanted to tell you, but it's a little strange. I'll save it for later, just between you and I."

She resumed reminiscing aloud to Grace.

⚜

Aurora lived the first few years of her life with her parents and baby brother in a cabin nicknamed The Shack in Chapsworth, Nebraska. Despite its peeling paint, slanting floors and persnickety wood stove, The Shack offered the young family indoor plumbing and a generous front porch spanning its width.

Shaded by towering trees' canopies and bordering a woodland area with a creek running through it, The Shack was just about the coolest place in town to fritter away a hot, muggy afternoon. It was often the hub of family gatherings, complete with grilled, blistered hot dogs, icy Coca-Cola in frosty green bottles, and creamy strawberry ice cream scooped out of the wooden hand crank freezer.

More importantly, The Shack was on the property of

Abel's Place, an entertainment complex owned by Aurora's grandfather, Abel McGregor. From 1940 to 1963, Abel's amusement park was a whizz-bang destination for people from many miles away, offering rides, parties and a roller skating rink – not to mention the furniture store, baseball fields and seasonal Christmas tree sales.

But the hands-down favorite attraction was the Merry-go-Round. The Coney Island style carousel was festooned with mirrored rounding boards sporting elaborate paintings of exotic people in faraway lands. Riders could either sit astride the gaudily painted horses or inside the beribboned chariots. The entire production was ablaze with dazzling lights, and the Wurlitzer pipe organ belted out popular music, summoning one and all to come and partake of the extravaganza.

Nestled in the wooded glen just beyond the park's Midway, The Shack always smelled faintly of burnt sugar and pungent mustard from cotton candy and hot dogs. Endless peals of mirth rang out from the Laughing Lady on the midway. With Mom or Dad hovering near, Aurora could toddle over to the Little Rebel Train or the Merry-Go-Round, and without fail, some park employee would scoop her up and hold her securely for a free ride.

Afterwards, they would carry her back home, a sleepyhead mess of pink, sugary goo and park dust. Clean and cuddly after a sponge bath and pyjamas, she would fall asleep to the sounds of distant laughter and thrilled screams, set to a background of calliope music carried on the wind.

Abel Loy McGregor, the son of a Scottish preacher who prided himself on knowing all the saints, was named for the "good" Biblical brother. He was also named for King Louis IX of France, the patron saint of architecture, who was canonized to sainthood in 1297 for his charitable works. It was hard to know whether Abel was simply born to success, or just strived extra hard to live up to his namesake. Either way, he savored every moment of his life.

A slender, wiry man in his younger years, Abel worked for a short time in a Missouri coal mine because he had the stamina to swing a pick ax for hours. However, the stifling darkness and confinement of the mine soon drove him back to Nebraska, where his high-school degree fulfilled the job requirement for teaching in a one-room country schoolhouse, and also helped local farmers with field work for spare cash on the side.

During a crisp Nebraska day, he helped load a truck with corn, danced a quick jig to amuse his buddy, and missed a step as he dismounted, falling and hitting his head on the pavement.

Everyone thought that Abel made a quick recovery, never knowing that when he fell off the truck, he damaged the pea-sized pituitary gland inside his head. This eventually led to his inexorable weight gain, which didn't slow until he topped out at three hundred pounds many years later.

But while he was still young and rakish, Abel aimed his

blue eyes and ornery grin at Daisy Griffith. She also had a preacher for a father, as well as four sisters, all of whom needed husbands. When Abel made his weekly courting visits to Daisy in her parents' front room, her baby sister, Camelia, found frequent excuses to "accidentally" amble in and linger like a high note in a choir until Daisy firmly escorted her out.

Abel found himself distracted by Camelia's petite beauty and chestnut hair that cascaded down to her knees, not to mention the occasional peek of her surprisingly red stockings. He'd never met anyone quite like her.

One night as Abel left the Griffiths' and headed for home, Camelia stepped out of the shadows under the willow tree and kissed him solid on the lips, then giggled and ran into the house.

After that, Abel couldn't stop thinking about her. He approached her father, offered his abject apologies for appearing fickle and humbly requested permission to call on Camelia, rather than Daisy.

Certainly Reverend Griffith would have preferred to marry off his older, plainer daughter, but at least he was relieving himself of one mouth to feed. So after some "time to consider," he reluctantly agreed, despite Daisy's wails and protests.

"You're nothing but a floozy, Camelia Griffith!" her older sister Grace exclaimed, as Daisy sobbed in her room. With their mother dead from a difficult childbirth, Grace had assumed the role of maternal authority in the household. "You should be ashamed of yourself!"

"Oh, be quiet, Grace! You're just jealous because the only beau you have is that hayseed, Hiram. All those muscles won't amount to much when all he can offer you is an old farm house and a lifetime of hard work."

Camelia spun around and huffed out, petticoats swishing against the door frame, leaving Grace to comfort her older sister and ponder her own future.

Abel and Camelia married. When the Great Depression tore the economy down, Abel opened a corner grocery store to ensure that his family would never lack food. Striking a shrewd balance between profit and charity, Abel drove himself and those around him with a ferocious intensity.

As his girth expanded, his corner store grew into a huge entertainment and retail complex. By 1942, Abel's Place was thriving, and continued to reign supreme as the entertainment capital in that corner of the Midwest for the next two decades.

Abel's employees were generally cowed by him. But with a child's keen perception, Aurora saw past his booming voice and brash demeanor and peered into his heart, which she found to be magnificent.

Beneath all his blunder and buss, Abel harbored a secret belief that it was up to adults to make the world better for children. He was disgusted that his granddaughter had been given a name she couldn't pronounce.

"She calls herself 'Awa' for pity sake! Sounds like the village idiot!" He insisted on calling her Bambi, after the storybook fawn.

One day she came skipping into Abel's living room, carrying a heap of yellow crinoline adorned with tiny, imitation lantana blossoms.

"Grandpa! Look! It's the most beautiful dress in the world!"

She stopped short, confused to find her huge grandpa outstretched on Camelia's green brocade couch, holding a puffy blue bag on his jaw.

"Are you sick?"

Abel's eyelids were heavy and his face ashen. "No, Bambi, I had some teeth pulled to make room for new teeth. I'm just a little sore. That's a beautiful dress, all right. I bet you look like a princess in it."

Aurora heard her mother and grandmother talking in hushed tones in the kitchen. "He had them all pulled, every one of them, all at once!" Camelia sounded peeved.

"What? Why on earth would he do that?"

"He said he wanted to get it over with and not have it drag on and on. The only time I saw him laid out like this was after he broke his pelvis and both his hips. He just has to do things all or nothing, you know how he is!" Camelia clucked her tongue. "And here I planned on waxing that floor today."

"Mom, have a heart! Did you give him some aspirin?"

"Of course, I've been waiting on him hand and foot. For such a big, strong man, he can sure be a big baby. He says the only thing that seems to help is that ice pack, and hot coffee. Makes no sense, if you ask me, but then he's a stubborn old coot."

"You're just so used to him taking care of everything and everyone, you don't know what to think when he needs taken care of."

The screen door slammed and their voices faded as they moved onto the front porch.

Aurora stuck her thumb in her mouth and regarded Abel as he laid his head back down and closed his eyes. She tucked her stuffed dog under his arm, laid down on the floor, and dozed off until her mother came in to take her home. He was gone for a while after that.

But a few weeks later, he appeared unannounced at the screen door of The Shack. He clicked his new dentures to made sure they were seated, and bellowed, "Put on that new dress, Bambi! We're having a party."

Aurora dropped her paper dolls, dashed into her bedroom and emerged carrying the frothy yellow dress.

"Help me, Mama!" Her mother sorted out the layers and helped her change clothes in the kitchen.

"Now remember, you can't wear this dress all the time. It's just for parties, otherwise it will get ruined."

Aurora gave a perfunctory nod and hurried back to the living room. Abel told her that sure enough, she did look like a princess, and reminded her to put on her shoes. Hollering their goodbyes to her mother, they climbed into Abel's pickup truck. For the rest of the afternoon, Aurora held court from behind Abel's shoulder at the skating rink's cash register, munching on fresh fried donuts and sipping lemonade.

⚜

Perched on the side of the well and swinging my feet like a ninny, I am lost in reminiscing about Abel when I realize, *Good grief! If I can hear this person, maybe she can hear me.*

I lean over and holler into the well, "Hey! I'm up here! I can hear you! Can you hear me?" I wait for some acknowledgment, but the voice drones on.

I try again, "Hey, you! You're talking about Abel McGregor, my brother-in-law. I'm up here, on top of the well!"

I listen again, as the voice keeps rambling.

She's calling him Grandpa Abel, and me Auntie Grace, why, I don't believe it, she must be little Aurora. Last I heard she's all grown up now, and teaching school.

I cup my hands over my mouth and once again yell down into the murky depths of the well. "Aurora! It's your Auntie Grace!"

I wait for a response, but Aurora's voice just keeps talking. "I'm not so sure how Grandpa got crippled," the voice says. I stiffen in annoyance.

"He wasn't crippled!" I object. "He was on wheels!"

She's got to stop and take a breath some time. I decide to just keep talking.

"There are two stories about how he got hurt. The first story is that Abel was playing another of his dang practical jokes. You know how annoyed Camelia used to get with him. Anyway, so the story goes, one night in 1942 Abel saw a friend riding the Ferris wheel, and thinking to tease him, pretended to grab his car as it went by.

"Just then, for some reason the mechanism shifted into the next gear and sped up, and Abel held on by instinct. Then he saw the ground falling away from him much too fast. He tried to keep his grip, but he weighed too much, and he fell, shattering his hips and pelvis."

I pause and listen. *Unbelievable! She doesn't even stop to take a breath!*

I turn up my own volume, "Aurora! Blabbermouth! I'm talking to you up here! About your grandpa!"

"The other version of the story is that Abel was removing cars from the Ferris wheel to prevent wind damage, and was holding on when the gears slipped, then it was too late to let go.

"Oh, we never knew for sure which story was true. The park employees liked to make Abel into a living legend or something. But I do know that afterwards, Abel complained of nightmares about trying to hang on to the wheel, and losing his grip one finger at a time until he fell to the ground."

The voice seems to have stopped.

So I continue, "The doctors in their stupidity said he would never walk again, but they didn't know him. He did manage to prove them wrong, but from then on he mostly sped around the park on a bright yellow scooter.

"Of course, being as how he was already heavy, he eventually gained so much weight that he had to obtain special permission from the government in Washington, D.C. to exceed the fabric allowance for his trousers during World War II! He was famous for so many reasons, not all of them good."

I laugh, shaking my head at the memory of Abel's escapades. "But honey, he just doted on you, and as I recall, the feeling was mutual."

⟡

Abel's yellow scooter became an accepted part of his notoriety and his injury didn't seem to stop him much. He and Camelia raised four daughters, and ran their thriving businesses. He could walk very short distances, his huge, arthritic hips rolling like a ship in rough seas. Usually though, he relied on the yellow scooter to travel all around the Park, giving him more speed and mobility than anyone else. People felt bad for what happened to him, but no one ever dared to call him crippled.

It was no secret that Aurora was the favored grandchild in her grandfather's Shangri-la. But the absolute best part of all her riches, the most prized treasure in her four-year-old world, was the yellow carousel horse.

Surely her horse was the most astounding example of equestrian splendor that ever graced this universe. Legs dazzling in an arrogant prance, he stood impossibly higher on his shiny brass pole than any of the other horses. His gleaming golden body was adorned with garish rococo garlands of flowers, mane and tail flourishing in an imaginary wind like lush saffron plumes on a rising phoenix bird.

And a face like no other! His nostrils flared with excitement beneath huge, flashing brown eyes and above his red mouth full of white teeth. He whinnied as if he planned to gallop directly to the stars and take his rightful place in the northern heavens alongside Pegasus.

There were no simpering mare's eyes here. He was her noble steed, her kindred spirit, her escape from the bonds of earth. When Aurora mounted the yellow horse and the ride picked up speed, it was no silly circle they traveled. Oh no. They were Sky Riders!

"I like the yellow horse the best, Mama."

"I know, honey. Do you have a name for him?"

"Grandpa Abel says his name is Pegasus. That's the name of a horse that was magic and lives in the stars now. I think my horse is magic, too."

And best of all, being Abel's granddaughter, she could request and keep the yellow carousel horse for as long as she liked.

One fine Indian summer afternoon, Aurora pushed her stool over to her closet and pulled the yellow party dress off its hanger. She slipped the fluffy layers over her head and ran out to greet her aunt's car just as it pulled into the yard. Her annoying cousin was making ugly faces at her through the side window. Her mother came around from the back at the same moment and frowned at her.

"It's for company, Mama! Can you please button it?"

While the adults settled into the kitchen, Aurora regarded her cousin, who squirmed in his new shirt and jeans like a katydid trying to shed its skin. She pranced up to him and twirled.

"How do you like my dress?"

He pointed at her and laughed, "You look like a big fuzzy duck."

Her mother hollered from the kitchen, "Go on now, you kids go outside and play. And take off that dress before you ruin it!"

Aurora sulked while her cousin picked at a mosquito bite. He perked up. "Wanna play Hide and Seek?"

She realized that this might be a way to avoid him for the rest of the afternoon. But it would be foolish to appear overly eager. She chewed on her lip and studied the ceiling for a minute. "Do you even know how to count?"

He scoffed. "Of course I can count, higher than you, I bet!"

"You have to count to 20. And don't skip numbers. And

you have to be 'It' first."They ran outdoors and he dutifully faced a tree, covered his eyes and began a labored count, "1...2...3...5...8...10...13...15...20...here I come!"

Aurora sped toward an extra special place to hide underneath the ramp in back of the roller skating rink, the one they used to load pianos into the furniture store. He would never find her! With one end set on the ground, and the other on a concrete block, it allowed just enough space for her to crawl in and curl up.

She hugged her knees to her chest, tucked the yellow crinoline underneath her, waited for her breath to become slow and quiet, and pecked out. No sign of him yet. Ha! She was going to surprise him! She waited, and waited, and waited some more, but still heard no sound of his approaching sneakered feet.

She was tired and thirsty, but didn't want to give up her favorite hiding place, so she stilled herself and nodded off to the lull of insects humming in the heat.

As the late afternoon shadows crept toward dinnertime, Aurora's aunt and cousin left in a flurry of behinds and elbows. He forgot to tell anyone about the game of Hide and Seek. With growing unease, her mom started asking around and checked the merry-go-round and the train. Alarmed that she still couldn't find Aurora, she alerted her husband and Abel.

In a matter of minutes, Abel gathered a search party. He pointed at each man as he shouted orders. "You check the rides! You try the baseball field! You run to the road, make sure she's not there! You check the skating rink! You there, are you listening? Get over to the furniture store. No, wait, head for the woods, I'll check the store. Get moving! Meet back here in 15 minutes, no more! Run!"

As they rushed through the park, the woods, the ball field, their shouts filled the air with her name, "Aurora!"

When they regrouped, breathless and forlorn, Abel swore and spat. "Call the police! Tell them we have a missing child!" Another hour passed as the police came to assist with searching, covering old ground with new care.

Still, Aurora continued sleeping, oblivious to the world and invisible to the eye.

But she wasn't invisible to a sensitive nose. The park abutted a woodland region active with wildlife. A family of coyotes roamed the area. The one that found her was two feet high and weighed nearly forty pounds, a scrappy male who had survived many adversaries as large as a little girl.

He was hungry.

He approached the child on soft paws, sniffed around her spot, and growled.

She woke with a start, arms and legs stiff from her cramped position. She opened her eyes and looked straight into the yellow eyes and snarling face of the coyote. His breath was foul and hot on her cheek. She screamed loudly just as the animal lunged for her throat. She put up her arm and tried to squeeze in further under the ramp. The coyote sunk its teeth into her wrist, scratching at the fabric of her dress for a foothold to pull her out. She tried to make her body as small as possible, to ball up completely under the ramp, away from those claws and teeth.

Abel was the closest and heard her screams.

He raced the yellow scooter at top speed toward the sound. He skidded around the corner behind the rink so fast that the scooter nearly toppled over.

He aimed his front wheel for the snarling coyote. The impact knocked the animal loose from Aurora, and sent its body sailing through the air, until it collided with the back wall of the skating rink and fell to the grass, neck broken.

She kept her eyes shut tight until the last moment, when she heard a loud bellow and high pitched shriek.

She opened them in time to see a blurred image of Grandpa Abel, huge against the setting sun, speeding by on a flash of furious yellow, sending the coyote flying. In her panic, she saw her grandfather flying up on Pegasus, her yellow carousel horse, to rescue her.

Bleeding and sobbing, she was unable to move. With his heart threatening to pound its way out of his chest, Abel called her name over and over. He dumped the scooter on the ground and tried to bend down to pick her up, but his size and his beleaguered hips were too much even for him.

"Come on out, Bambi! You can do it! Grandpa's here, you're OK now." His voice was unsteady, but reassuring. She slowly crawled out of her best hiding place, and into his arms.

The doctor gave her twenty-two stitches, but at least she didn't need rabies shots. For the next few months, she loudly insisted that Grandpa Abel had rescued her on Pegasus, her golden horse, no matter how many times the adults tried to convince her of the truth.

Finally, Abel said, "Hell's bells, let her alone, there's nothing wrong with a kid believing in a magical horse."

Shortly after her fifth birthday, Aurora's dad got a better job, one with a possibility of moving upward into management. The family relocated from Chapsworth to Bloomingdale, about an hour to the north.

Over the next several years, Aurora's preoccupation with the yellow horse was outpaced by more pressing concerns such as kindergarten, hopscotch, learning to dog paddle and ride her tricycle, then bicycle, and the arrival of another baby brother.

Meanwhile, the health of Abel and all that he had created was declining. People were spending more time in front of their televisions, or on long road trips in their new cars. Park attendance and profits steadily declined.

The final blow to Abel's entertainment domain came in the form of another type of "eminent" domain, when the state purchased his land for ten percent of its true commercial value in order to make room for a new highway.

When her family made a Christmas visit to Chapsworth, Aurora asked to see the park. In disbelief, she regarded the concrete roadway and acres of dirty snow occupying the space that used to be Abel's jubilee.

"Where did the rides go?" she wailed. "Where is the merry-go-round with my yellow horse? The roller skating rink? The furniture store? The Shack? What will Abel do?"

"Abel's retired, honey," her mother tried to reassure her. "He's going to take it easy now."

"That's a load of hooey! Abel never did anything "easy" in his life."

Abel's health continued to weaken. He had his scooter, but no purpose or destination.

No one needed him any more to schedule the parties, purchase supplies, set up the rides, skating rink or food concessions, round up the crew, open the doors, welcome the customers, patrol the Midway, man the cash register, or make the magic happen.

This giant of a man who once ruled his Midwestern Mecca from the seat of a yellow scooter became the unthinkable. *Obsolete,* he cringed as he tried the word out in his mind. *I've become obsolete, that's the truth of it. Hell's bells, I'm as useless as that silly carousel horse that Aurora used to love so much.*

One day in 1975, they received a phone call.

Abel had died of a heart condition.

But Aurora knew that Abel's colossal heart never skipped a beat. It simply got broken.

"I still can't believe he's gone," Aurora murmured, shaking her head. Lily took her hand. "I know, honey, he had so much life in him."

"Well, that leads up to what I was wanting to tell you earlier.

"A few years after Abel died, my folks took us on a road trip to San Francisco. We visited an abandoned amusement park near the old Sutro Bathhouse. It was a decrepit place. There was still a Laughing Sal, a Hall of Mirrors full of litter, and these rusted out rides. Anyway, it got me to thinking about Abel's Place.

"That night I dreamed an eight-foot-tall version of him, dressed in a long-sleeved black shirt with beads and fringe, black leather pants, ornate black cowboy boots, and a black ten-gallon hat with shiny silver ornaments. He was riding a huge palomino with dark eyes and flared nostrils. I could see the muscles rippling, and sparks flying from his hooves, just like I used to imagine Pegasus.

"Anyway, Abel winked at me, same as he always did, and rode off into this ridiculously gorgeous sunset right out of Hollywood." She laughed and caricatured a large wink. "It made me happy, thinking about him out there riding around the cosmos, having a fine old time.

"So then I kind of moved on. Grew up, got married, moved to Lincoln, had two kids, and started teaching kindergarten. You know how time flies and all that.

"Just lately, after I heard about Auntie Grace being in a coma and decided to come visit, I was reading my students a story about a cowboy hero and his magical horse. Then I told them to put some pictures about the story into their journals, and circulated around the classroom while they drew and colored.

"All of the kids depicted the cowboy and the horse in their own versions, some with orange, others with purple, you know how kids like to color. All except one. 'Billy,' I said, 'that's a wonderful picture! Are you going to add some more colors?'

"He just ignored me and added wings to his solid yellow horse. I had this sudden image of being five years old again, my legs gripping that silly carousel horse while we whirled past the crowd and I pretended we were flying. Meanwhile, Billy added a black hat with silver ornaments to his cowboy, who was already dressed all in black, even black boots.

"I asked him, 'Is that the same cowboy from the story?' He shook his head and frowned. 'That's my hero,' he corrected me. 'He's better than that guy in the story. He and the yellow horse ride around and help people. I saw him one time, when my brother hit his head diving into the pond, and I couldn't swim yet, the hero made an air bubble so he could breathe until my Dad got there.'

"Tell you what, Aunt Lily, I got shivers up my spine when he said that. I still don't know what to think."

"Well, here's what I think. There's lots of things we can't explain, but if anyone can live beyond the grave, it would be Abel. I kind of hope it's true."

❧❖❧

My Stars, I can't believe she doesn't hear me!

As I realize that Aurora's voice is making sounds of departure, I look around for a small rock to throw down the well.

I'll just have to risk bashing her in the head. She seems pretty hard headed anyway, probably got that from her grandpa.

I lean over into the well's dank coolness, marveling again at the strange water, and toss in the rock. It vanishes into thin air, without any hint of a splash.

Dang! I repeat this experiment with a few larger rocks, but the results are the same. Deflated, I turn and slump back to the hammock beneath the oak tree. Eureka sits in the shade, tongue hanging out as he pants to stay cool.

"What was I thinking? I'm in a dream, and I can't expect things to make sense. It's no big surprise that there's an annoying well in my yard where I can hear people, but they can't hear me, and the water shines and shimmers, but it doesn't reflect, or even splash.

"I really need to wake up. Tomorrow I'm going to try and get back into my body and wiggle my toes or something. This is a fun dream, but I'm tired of being locked out of my own world. Besides, I really miss everybody."

I fall into a fretful doze, with Eureka burrowing into the crook of my neck, and the steady hum of bees from my hives nearby.

Chapter 5

Honeycomb

1985

"mmm ..."

"Mom? Was that you? Mom, are you trying to talk? Nurse! Nurse!"

"What is it? Is something wrong?

"I think my mother tried to talk!"

"Really! What did she say?"

"Well, she kind of hummed."

"Oh, honey, that's not unusual when folks are in a vegetative state. It usually doesn't mean they're waking up."

Lily glares and the nurse sighs.

"But I'll check that she's all tucked in and cozy, just to make sure she's okay."

For what seems like the hundredth time, I will my toe to wiggle. It doesn't have to twirl around, just enough to nudge the blanket so that someone will notice.

The nurse is fussing with the covers, this is perfect timing.

But somewhere between my mind and my toe, there is

a disconnect. Nothing happens.

No matter, it's a long way from brain to toe. Maybe someplace closer in, like a finger.

Okay, never mind the finger. Maybe an eyelid?

Just a dadgum eyelid! Flicker! Hurry up! She's leaving.

Nothing. It's so disheartening. I can hear Lily starting to cry. Again. It pains me so to hear my daughter grieving, and it's my fault.

And the diabolically soft, relentless snowflakes are starting to crowd my thoughts already. Even more worrisome, I have the uneasy sense that people are doing things to my body, some of which seem normal, and others not so much.

I've lived in the world long enough to know that sometimes there are predators where you least expect them.

But no matter how much I try to stay alert, I can't quite tell exactly who they are or what they're doing.

Defeated, I drift back to the portal and ease my way into my kitchen in Possibilities, where Eureka is napping. I can't help it. I just have to go check back at the well.

Hearing Aurora's voice from below made me really homesick.

Maybe the well is like a kind of crossroads, where my dream and the real world meet up.

So I spend the better part of a day (a week? a month?) listening at the well, and yelling, cursing, even screaming into the coolness to elicit some kind of response.

No one answers.

It's just the loneliest feeling, talking to people who don't answer.

Hearing nothing but your own echo.

"I don't know, Jessica. Maybe I'm starting to imagine things. I could've sworn it sounded like a meaningful 'mmm.' Trying to keep some hope while being realistic about Mom's prospects feels like speeding up and stopping at the same time. I'm an emotional wreck."

The nurse patted Lily's shoulder. "I know. I can only imagine what a strain this is on you and the family."

"If only life could stand still until she recovers. But instead we have to keep up with all the normal routines and demands, and after a while, people forget that we're living a nightmare that doesn't end.

"Even we forget! Sometimes I dream that none of this has happened. That Mom died and we buried her and we're moving on. Then I wake up and it hasn't ended, and I don't know how the world turned so upside down."

"I'm so sorry, honey. I am truly sorry. She never deserved this, no one does. But I can guarantee you she's not suffering. We're taking good care of her, and I'm sure that at some level, she knows you're here."

"It's just that she was like the hub of our wheel. She connected all our various parts and people, and now the wheel is wobbling along all catawampus."

Jessica hugged her. "I know she found comfort in her religious beliefs, didn't she? I don't mean to sound trite, but does prayer help you? It sure helped me when my baby boy died in his sleep a few years back."

"If only I knew what to pray for. Her recovery? Or her release?"

"What do you think she would want if she could tell you now?"

"I wish I knew," Lily shook her head, "I just wish to God I knew."

That was the real irony of it all.

All her life, Grace had been a superb listener. But somehow, either she hadn't talked, or no one had listened. No one could say for certain what she would want them to do.

They had always just assumed she would die peacefully in her sleep. Who ever imagines their loved ones with tubes in their stomach, wearing diapers, developing bedsores, and wasting away in a surreal limbo, unable to move or speak?

One thing was clear to everyone; as time wore on, the Grace they loved was fading away. It was as if her very essence was dissolving into the air of the room.

"Oh, sure, I have you, Eureka, and you're very smart for a dog, and good company, but I'm lonesome for some human company. Having someone to visit with would keep my mind off of worrying."

I wonder ... I shake my head. It's too outrageous.

Still ... *I wonder if I could bake up some people. Oh my Lord, that sounds horrible when I put it into words. I couldn't do it.*

I start holding imaginary conversations with family members and close friends, inventing their lines and saying them aloud in my best imitation of their voices.

Not only is this unsatisfying, but it's giving me the heebie-jeebies.

"I haven't had imaginary friends since I was three years old. Why don't I just reconstitute Santa Claus and the Easter Bunny, while I'm at it?"

The puppy whined.

"Don't worry, I'm kidding."

So I stop talking to specters from my memories. And the heavy ache of loneliness grows to be a constant burden, weighing down my spirit.

Reluctantly, I decide there is no real harm in trying to bake a person.

After all, this whole thing is imaginary, really.

I resolve to start with a friend who is already dead and buried. Making a copy of someone who is still alive, or even a dead family member, would feel downright ghoulish.

Of all my deceased acquaintances, there is one who fits the bill. My long time friend and neighbor, Doris Hansen from down the road ... remember I mentioned earlier how she brought me home a couple of times when I got lost? Well, she had a stroke just before they put me into the nursing home. Died quick and painless, lucky girl.

It's not like I'm going to be disturbing her or anything, I reassure myself, I'm just creating a doughy copy of her to keep me company.

Nonetheless, I can't help shivering a little as I ease into a kitchen chair and pick up a wad of dough.

I mold a copy of Doris based on a fond memory of her. I sing a song about friends and neighbors and watch with mixed horror and fascination as the dough takes shape and fleshes out into a plump, disheveled woman in a flouncy hat, carrying one of those large, flowered straw purses nearly half her size.

I recall her daughter bought that purse for her on a trip to Florida. I thought it was a monstrosity, but she carried it with her everywhere.

The lifelike dough woman bustles over to the mirror on the wall, with several of her body parts jiggling in opposite directions.

Despite my misgivings, I can't help but feel secretly proud.

It looks just like her!

I watch in delight as my newly created Dough-Doris refreshes her lipstick, tugs her seersucker dress taut over her bounteous bosom, and lets out a belch.

"Shoot! I just hate wearing this girdle contraption in the

summer! Gives me gas. Well, don't just stand there, Gracie May, we're late for church. Let's get crackin'!"

I have a sharp pang of doubt. *What if being lonely was God's way of testing me, and I failed miserably?*

"Where did this hot dog puppy come from? Isn't he just the cutest thing? GRACE!"

I jump up and pin a white lace handkerchief on top of my hair. As I help my dough friend down the stairs to the screen door, I marvel at the lifelike flesh of her arm.

Doris's bustling departure after church leaves me wondering about more than where the heck is she going.

In fact, now I'm in a real quandary.

It hasn't all seemed too bad. In fact, it's pretty satisfying to have someone to be with, even if I can't be completely honest with Dough-Doris. The truth is, I feel better.

"You would think that baking up a person is the most natural thing in the world!" I assure Eureka, who ignores me in favor of his new bone. "Huh. Maybe it's not such a big deal, after all. I mean what a lame idea, to think that I could bake real people."

Lame or not, it feels good to have someone around to talk to. There is a limit to how far you can carry one-way conversations, like those I have with Eureka or the voices at the well.

I decide to bake more people, but only after some tough deliberations.

Should I make them old or young? After all, I'd rather see them young and attractive, not old and sickly. Now that I think of it, I'm feeling pretty young myself. Fearing that the well's lack of reflection means I've become invisible, I tentatively step in front of the mirror.

"Sakes Alive!" I gasp at the pretty young woman with wavy, dark hair who stares back at me with her clear, green eyes.

"It's me! Woohoo! It's me in my 20's!" I run to pick up Eureka and waltz him around the kitchen. Then set him down and do a jitterbug. Unbelievable. But who's to say what's real anymore?

And so what if it isn't?

That decides it. I create a few more of my dough friends with their youth restored, and send them off to their respective homes or somewhere down the road, I guess.

Then I run into the bedroom, throw on my favorite white sundress and straw hat, and run out the screen door, with Eureka just barely scurrying out before it slams him from behind. We jump into the Phaeton and head full throttle into town.

In a flurry of renewed dough mixing and molding, I create all kinds of people, placing them throughout Possibilities so that it becomes a "living" town. We have families, tradespeople and shopkeepers, police, firemen and administrators, and (with mild regret on my part), uppity lawyers and politicians.

Then I sit down on a park bench and enjoy the scene.

"This is more like it, Eureka. This is what a town should be."

Office people eating their brown bag lunches, mothers with their babies in strollers, children and dogs pestering the pigeons, ducks on the little lake, it's so wonderful.

Too bad there wasn't this beautiful little park in my real farm community, we could have so enjoyed it.

I'm watching a little girl in a pink tutu showing off her ballet steps to her mother, "Look, Mommy! See what I learned?"

Watching her, I don't realize that I'm humming an old melody from a Fred Astaire and Ginger Rogers movie.

Weren't they just elegance in motion?

As I hum, the air around me starts to shimmer and vibrate.

Uh oh. Now what?

The vibration intensifies, competes with my humming until it merges with the melody and seems to permeate the air around me.

I feel myself dissolving, melting. There is a slight jolt, like a gear has slipped somewhere, and the scene before me changes.

I am looking up at the young girl's mother smiling down at me. I can feel the girl's feet moving, and hear her voice talking, but strangest of all, I seem to be tucked into her thoughts.

Like I have slipped into a honeycomb where she and I are meshed together.

Then, just as abruptly, I return to find Eureka watching me quizzically.

"Did you see that? Did you see me go somewhere? I kind of dissolved or something."

He lays his head on his paws and regards me with what I swear looks like doubt.

I check all my fingers and toes, determine that I am complete, and wonder if I can make the dissolving happen again. I look across the park, see a man swimming in the lake, and hum the "fishies swimming" tune.

Again, the vibration, the little jolt, the sense of a gear slipping or a wheel missing a cog, and then I am dissolving and merging into a space ... or something ... between his thoughts.

Feeling like a trespasser, and not so keen on fishing, I quickly retreat.

"Eureka! I can dissolve my thoughts into the spaces in between other people's thoughts, like inside a honeycomb, you know? Huh. I wonder if maybe that's how those psychics at the fair tell your fortune?

"Hiram always said they were frauds, but maybe there are people in real life who somehow get into the spaces between your thoughts. Or maybe that's how psychologists and counselors do their work. I sure wish I could talk with my Iris about this; she's studying to be a psychologist, you know.

"Anyway, I don't know about the right and wrong of

it. Values and rules seem to be a little sketchy in my dream here. After all, I made these dough people, didn't I? But it still seems a little intrusive, don't you think?

"Maybe if I don't disturb the honeycomb or steal anything, and I keep really quiet…if I just dissolve right into the spaces in between."

The dog scratches intently behind his ear.

"This could be really fun, Eureka. I always wanted to know what it would be like to be this person or that one."

I start slowly at first. Don't even know what to call it. Honeycomb hitchhiking? Thought trespassing? Losing my mind? That last one seems the most likely.

In any case, not to sound ungrateful, but it really does take some strain and effort. At first if I stay too long, I get a headache.

Maybe it will get easier with practice. Like jumping on a pogo stick. Took me ages to learn that.

"It really is kind of like hitchhiking, right Eureka? Oh, I know, they're not really inviting me into their car, but on the other hand, I'm not doing any true harm. Just trying out some ideas that are different from my own.

"Like trying orange sherbet just for the fun of it, even though your favorite will always be vanilla."

Perfecting this new process occupies my time for a while (an hour? a month?). It's not like I have much else to do.

I lose count how many times it takes, but finally I learn

to concentrate hard and focus my thoughts.

It's a lot like threading a needle. Get focused, calm the mind, steady the hand. But what fun! This makes walking a mile in their shoes seem like yesterday's news.

Over time, it gets easier, but I still pace myself.

One day, as I'm cutting some fresh broccoli stalks in the garden, I hear a voice through the kitchen window, coming from the well. I run outside and hurry over to listen. It sounds like my old school chum, Ginny. She was a constant help to me through so many hard times, and she remained hale and hearty even as I got sick and decrepit.

"Abigail's in trouble," Ginny's voice is pleading with God, it sounds like. "I'm afraid something terrible is happening and she won't tell anyone."

My heart goes chilly. Abigail is my goddaughter. I have to try and help. But how? I feel as useless as a two-legged chair.

I nuzzle Eureka's warm body in my arms as an idea blossoms in my imagination. *No, it's impossible*

Maybe not.

Yes, it is. And wrong. Very, very wrong.

Just in and out. Quick like a bunny. Find out what's going on and take it from there.

Anyway, I can't do it.

Won't know 'til you try.

Who are you, anyway?

I'm you, silly, you're arguing with yourself. And wasting time.

The dog squirms to get down and I let him.

"Eureka, what if I can dissolve into the thoughts of people who are alive? What if that's a way I can make myself heard? Imagine! I could communicate with Lily and Luke and Iris and everyone!"

He yelps.

"Yes, it sounds crazy farfetched. I can't even wag a finger in the real world. But if there's a way I can make my thoughts be heard, I need to try. Besides, Ginny was a wonderful friend to me, and Abby is my goddaughter. I have a responsibility."

I focus hard on Ginny's prayer, and picture Abigail in my mind. She always reminded me of Alice in Wonderland, with her delicate features and blonde hair, and she'd be all grown up now. I hum a little, focus a lot, feel the gears slip, then myself dissolving, and I slip into the honeycomb spaces of Abby's thoughts.

This is my first big mistake.

⚜

Steve won Abby's heart the first time she saw him, helping an elderly man in a wheelchair at the grocery store.

After a few flirty conversations in the produce section, they exchanged phone numbers, and she felt all warm inside when he called her.

He was a handsome young entrepreneur, although she wasn't so clear about what kind of business he ran. Real estate? Import/export? Something like that.

He threw money around like he had an endless supply. Their courtship was a dizzying frolic of dining and dancing at all the best nightclubs in town. Steve was a talented dancer. Sometimes they just walked in, signed up for a dance contest at the last minute, and breezed into first place. As she spun across the floor in his arms, Abby felt like the whole world became a sparkling disco ball.

That same synergy played out in their lovemaking, and Abby felt beautiful and seductive for the first time in her life. Steve's passion for everything, including her, seemed inexhaustible.

"He's perfect!" she gushed to her best friend, Mary. "He reminds me of that hero cowboy in an old TV series my parents used to watch."

"Who and what?"

"You know, that guy on the old western, not Roy Rogers, the other one, always wore black, lived high on the hog, incredibly sexy?"

"Oh, yeah, I vaguely remember him. I liked him, too. Definitely more appealing than John Wayne or Clint Eastwood."

"Truly. I couldn't stand those 'aw shucks ma'am,' stubborn as a mule cowboys who looked stoic to cover up their stupidity. This guy was like one of the knights of old, smart and gallant. An adventurer, champion, daredevil, a protector who rode in on horseback to save the day."

"That's a pretty tall order, even for a cowboy."

Abby rolled her eyes. "Anyhow, Steve reminds me of that guy, that's my point. He's my hero."

At that, Mary rolled her eyes in imitation and groaned, "Geez, Abby, you've got it bad."

Steve and Abby were married in a small ceremony in Red Rock Canyon, and celebrated their honeymoon in San Francisco. She thought she was the luckiest girl in the world. After they returned to Las Vegas, Abby resumed her work as a flight attendant for Western Skies, a small regional airline with DC-9 jets. Usually gone for two or three days at a time, she couldn't wait to get back home to Steve.

He purchased their first house in a new, exclusive suburb near Henderson, Nevada, and moved their belongings into the home while she was away at work, leaving her a message about where to come when she returned to Las Vegas. The two-story home was decked out with all the latest fixtures, vaulted ceilings, a wet bar, even a small elevator and a pool.

Abby contemplated the sterile white walls as she hung her grandmother Ginny's antique clock in the living room. "This place really needs some color," she thought, and fell asleep over a pile of home decorating magazines.

"You're not really going to hang that there, are you?" She woke to find Steve frowning from the doorway.

She stretched and sat up, still drowsy. "My grandmother gave it to me, it's one of my favorite things."

"It's just that it doesn't really go with anything. How about if we put it in the spare room?"

"It tick-tocks."

He smiled, "Good, so guests won't overstay their welcome."

Abby moved the clock and went out to pick up a paint color wheel.

During their third month together, she began to have more serious doubts. He had been staying out all night once or twice each week. He seemed to not need sleep. When she asked him, "Where were you all night? Who were you with?" he always had a litany of places, and friends' names, which he linked to "commercial real estate."

"We have to show these properties after hours, the landlords and owners want to keep things private. Besides, these things take schmoozing, baby, and that usually happens in nightclubs, where everyone's drinking and having fun. It's just business, and isn't it great we are making so much money?"

Abby had to admit the money was nice. She tucked away her doubts (was he dealing drugs?) and decided to enjoy the fact that life seemed as good as the Fourth of July.

"I don't know, Mary, maybe I'm asking for too much. What should be expected from marriage, really?" she wondered aloud, as they lounged by the pool, sipping margaritas.

Mary, who relished her independence, didn't miss a beat. "I see it like this. There are two things. First, your spouse should be your very best friend, I mean *very* best friend, better than all your girlfriends.

"Second, both of you, not just him, should have better lives together than you would have apart. The reason I'm still single is because I haven't found a man who meets both those conditions."

Abby stewed. Steve was a good friend in many respects. In fact, he could be positively glowing in his praise, as well as very loving towards her. He always encouraged her to do whatever she liked.

So why couldn't she shake off this foreboding that something was very wrong?

Maybe it was his temper. Steve's passion wasn't limited to making love or making money. His temper could explode out of nowhere, for no reason, and with little warning.

"I can't find my gold hoop earrings; have you seen them?"

"Jesus, Abby, can't you stop pestering me? I'm not in charge of your goddamn earrings! They make you look like a frickin' hooker, anyway."

He's just tired, and he has a lot on his mind; I need to not bother him when he's working out deals. Besides, he always makes it up to me with jewelry or a treat.

But she never could really tell when he was working,

and it was hard not to take his comments to heart. Over time, even though the presents were valuable and fun, they started to feel like guilt offerings.

She found herself putting up emotional antennae to avoid antagonizing him, tiptoeing around his unpredictable mood swings. As the months passed, it became increasingly difficult to resist believing the terrible criticisms he flung at her when enraged.

No matter how much Abby tried to appease or sidestep his moods, the outbursts grew worse. Blame and accusations lathered with obscenities became the norm. She began to feel frightened of Steve's temper.

One night Abby dreamed that a presence, like a subtle shift in energy, had come into her awareness. She awoke feeling fuzzyheaded, unable to shake the notion that somehow she wasn't alone.

"It's weird, Steve, I had this dream about a guardian angel or something, taking up residence in my subconscious. So weird." She sipped her coffee and laughed.

His mood was conciliatory, in contrast to his temper of the night before. "Leave it to you to think of guardian angels, baby. You know, I think you are my guardian angel," Steve crooned to her as he quickly kissed her forehead and headed out the door. She wondered how long it would be before he turned once again from happy and loving to irrational and belligerent. She felt her muscles and mind relax at the prospect of having some solitude at home.

❧❖❧

I wish I could be your guardian angel, Abby, I think maybe you need one. Seems like you've gone from walking on air to walking on glass. I wonder if I should try to call out or something, but I feel like such an intruder, tucked away inside a real person's thoughts. So I hunker down and wait for a chance to do something.

❧❖❧

It was a warm Las Vegas evening when Steve punched Abby for the first time. There was the hickory scent of grilled burgers in the air, the hiss of rotating lawn sprinklers and Kenny Rankin's cool jazz wafting from the stereo in the living room.

"Babe, can you bring out the catsup?" he asked her, as she sliced onions and tomatoes in the kitchen.

She looked in the refrigerator, then the cupboard.

"Sorry, we're out."

The silence went on for too long. She turned to find his angry hulk blocking out the light in the doorway.

"You stupid bitch! Didn't you buy any?"

Abby flushed with anger. "I've been gone for three days on a flight! You could have shopped for groceries."

"I can't do frickin' everything around here!"

He took one giant step forward, then his fist impacted her jaw, snapping her head back. Abby stood in utter shock for a few seconds before she crumpled to the floor in pain and shock. She felt him kick her ribs as she lost consciousness.

She had the dizzying sense of being sick and immobilized in a dark room, with a tube protruding from her stomach. She could hear canned laughter from a television show in the room next door.

When a large shadow crossed the sliver of light shining in from the parking lot, she realized that she wasn't alone. She felt a heavy weight settle onto her bed. A sweaty hand made its way up her pajama leg and rested, to her horror, on her thigh.

⚜

From my hiding place in Abby's mind, I am sharply yanked into her nightmare. *Or wait. Is this my own nightmare?* The edges where my thoughts meet Abby's are getting sticky and blurred. I try to pull away, return to my own awareness, but I am dazed from Steve's beating, and can't focus. Getting hit in the face and kicked in the ribs is a lot worse than they make it look in the movies.

⚜

Abby wondered if Steve was fondling her. She couldn't move, or speak. She felt locked into her body. The hand was probing. Then she heard the sound of a zipper being undone, felt pressure on her pelvis. An intrusive fullness. Revolted and terrified, she woke up, heart pounding, each gasping breath racking her sides with sharp pain. She wondered if Steve had broken one of her ribs. But at least she was back in her own bedroom. And Steve was gone. She was safe. For now.

Chapter 6

Lost and Found

Tumbling around in some kind of thought storm, I wrap my arms tightly around my knees and try to get upright. I know that Steve is gone, so Abby must be safe.

So why do I feel so nauseated? Where am I? Who is being molested?

I try to focus my thoughts in Possibilities but can't seem to locate the resonance. I begin to panic.

What if I can't get back? What if I'm stuck here for eternity?

Steve's tantrums worsened. So did the beatings. Sometimes Abby hid at Mary's house until she had to leave for work.

"I can't keep hiding from him, Mary. First of all, I can't live out of a suitcase forever. Secondly, this puts you in danger, if he comes looking for me here. I don't want to put anyone else in his way when he's mad."

"Leave him! This is getting too dangerous."

"And go where? The Mission?"

"My friend in Phoenix says they have a shelter for women who are getting beat up at home."

"I wish we had one here. But we don't. And anyway, it would just delay the inevitable. I need to find an apartment and get a divorce."

"Why should you have to move? Get a restraining order and kick him out!"

"It costs $100 for a restraining order and lots more than that for a lawyer. And how am I going to evict him? Not only that, I made a vow to my friends and family, and to God, in sickness and in health, for better or for worse. How can I betray that vow?"

"God never meant for you to be injured in your own home. I think that's an unspoken loophole, don't you? At least tell your brothers and let them beat the crap out of him."

"What good would that do? I don't dare tell anyone, and you can't either. He has a gun, and he has dangerous friends, and I don't want to be the cause of anyone else getting hurt. I'm trying to stay out of his way until I can figure out how to leave. It makes me sad, though. I know it's just drugs doing this to him."

"At least you're finally admitting that his money is dirty. Drug money. That makes him all the more dangerous, Abby."

Despite the thorny logistics of doing everything in secret, Abby rented an apartment, set up a new phone and utilities, and starting sneaking a few boxes over at a time.

But one night as she was leaving the new apartment,

Steve ambushed her at the door, wild-eyed and yelling, brandishing his gun. He reeked of Canadian Club and looked like he hadn't shaved in days.

She screamed and cried as he twisted her arm behind her, pushed her back inside and face down on the couch, then planted his knee in her back.

"You think you can run away from me? You stupid cow! You think I'm that easy to fool?" She felt something cold and hard against the base of her skull. "Feel that? You'd better hope it's your lucky day, because we're going to play a new game. It's called 'Hope to God the Chamber is Empty'."

In horror, she heard a click and realized he was holding a gun to her head, and pulling the trigger. "There's only one unlucky chamber, sweetheart, let's see if it's the next one."

Abby struggled to free herself but was held fast by her twisted arm, and his knee in her back, like a bug impaled on a collector's pin.

"Oh my God, Oh my God, Oh my God," she prayed desperately, eyes squeezed shut.

Click.

"Oh, lucky girl so far."

Abby had an insane thought that maybe she wasn't going to die, because her life wasn't flashing before her eyes the way people said it did.

Click.

Three chambers gone. She struggled harder, tried to kick him as he twisted her arm higher and dug in his knee.

Then she had a traitorous thought about how easy it would be to surrender. To just let him take what he wanted. Her life. Just give it up, stop this insanity, cheat him by dying. That would serve him right!

Click.

Just then, a siren. A blessed siren. The sound of men yelling, pounding on her door. The pressure on her arm and back suddenly released, and she heard the gun drop to the floor with a dull thud as Steve rushed out the back door. Frantic, she sobbed to the police officers, "Please, please arrest him!"

They did, but were only able to hold Steve for one night until he made bail. By that time, Abby had hurriedly dumped her most precious belongings into large sheets and tied the corners together, hobo style, called a cab, and talked her new landlord into giving her an apartment in a different complex across town.

❈

Remember I told you there were some hard parts to my story? I really, really hate to tell you this, but you deserve to know all of it, so you understand that things can get better no matter how bad they are.

As I struggle to free myself from Abby's thoughts and return to Possibilities, my nurse at Sunset Suites struggles to wrap her mind around a terrible truth.

Someone on staff has been abusing the female residents.

At night. When no one else is around. Some of the ladies, like me, are pretty much unconscious, so they couldn't yell for help even if someone was close enough to hear. Others report it, but are dismissed as demented or deluded.

Did I know? Of course I knew. I may be in a coma, and I may be occupying my time in an imaginary world, but I'm not a moron. Every time, I hope and pray that he'll get caught. But mostly I hope and pray that my family doesn't learn of it. They've already been through enough.

Anyway, they've figured out it's the new orderly, who was hired a few months back. The Medical Director has ordered that the man be placed on immediate suspension without pay, pending a full investigation.

Which is fine, except that in the meanwhile, I am curled up in a remote corner of Abby's thoughts. Memories of the orderly are interspersed with flashes of pain and terror. Somehow Abby and I got our nightmares mixed up, and I've lost my way.

I knew this was a bad idea!

I huddle for a time, then begin to wander aimless and confused through a sticky web of tangled emotions and memories.

❦

"He did *what*? Lily! What did you say?" Michael's voice, normally modulated, roared from the receiver.

Lily winced as she held onto her composure with a vice

like grip.

"He molested her, Michael. At night while she was asleep. And apparently it wasn't just her. A few of the old ladies were talking about it, but no one took them seriously. Everyone here is horrified, of course, and they've started a group lawsuit, however you call that. I've signed on, of course. I figure you can take over that piece, if you don't mind."

Dead silence. She continued, feeling as though her words were empty, futile. How could any of this be real? Unable to speak more of the unspeakable, she resorted to a neutral narrative.

"I don't mean this to sound ludicrous or grisly, but there doesn't seem to be a noticeable change in Mom's overall condition. We've moved her to a place called Elegant Manor. It's further away, and it seems nice enough, but Luke and I plan to trade off visiting at odd hours, even in the middle of the night, for a while, just to be sure. Also, do you remember Ginny's son, Philip? He's the Manager there, and he promised to keep her safe."

Michael gripped the phone and choked back his rage. This wasn't Lily's fault, but he knew she felt responsible.

"Thank God you got her out of there. And absolutely we're going to sue. I just wish I could deal with that worm shit myself." His voice broke. "It's the first time I'm glad she's unconscious. I haven't been the greatest son in terms of being there."

Lily started to cry. "She was so proud of you, when you got your broker's license and moved to New York. We're all proud of you, Michael. But if you can make time to come and see her, it might be a good idea. I know she would love to hear your voice."

"Does she respond to anyone's voice?"

Lily paused. "No, not really, but sometimes I feel like her expression changes, just slightly, as if she's trying to let us know she hears us or something. I just can't give up on her, that's all."

"I'll try to carve out some time next month to fly back."

Lily knew he meant well, and was equally sure that he wouldn't be coming. Michael had never been one to hang around when people were sick, or even unlucky. He seemed to think that adversity was contagious.

No sense in blaming him, even though it seemed a form of cowardice. He was paying for Grace's hospitalization, and thank God for that, because otherwise they couldn't afford it. *Not that money has guaranteed her safety*, Lily thought grimly. Aloud, she said, "Just come when you can, Michael. We love you."

"I love you, too. Keep me informed, OK? I'll be sending an attorney out there to take deposition statements, so don't be intimidated, just tell the whole story."

"I will." Lily hung up the phone, ran into the bathroom and vomited. She splashed cold water on her face, and regarded her reflection under the greenish flourescent light as she dried off and blew her nose.

How do you like that? I look older than Mom. Her bitter laugh gave way to deep sobs.

⚜

With the help of the Legal Aid agency, Abby filed for divorce. Then she relocated to the Western Skies crew base in Seattle. Memories of Steve's abuse continued to haunt her in the form of flashbacks and nightmares.

She never felt quite safe anywhere.

She enrolled in a karate class. Over the subsequent weeks and months, her skills improved until one day her instructor told her, "You can be a ferocious fighter. Stop holding back."

One night, Abby returned from a twelve-hour day of full flights. She was bone weary, hungry, still in her flight uniform, cutting up chicken as it heated in the frying pan. She heard a knock on her door, and hurried to answer, expecting a package from back home. When she opened the door, she gasped and fell backwards, terrified.

Steve's silhouetted face and large form engulfed her doorway. He lunged towards her, glowering, rolling up his sleeves.

"How dare you? How dare you leave me? Me! When I'm done with you, nobody will want you!"

Her thoughts raced as she struggled against hopelessness. How had he found her? She had been so careful to cover her tracks. Moved to a different city. Started using her middle name. Got an unlisted phone and address.

Maybe he wasn't human at all, but a succubus of the devil, reaching out with tentacles to suck her soul dry.

She was so tired. Tired of fighting, running, hurting and feeling like a fool and a failure. Tired of looking over her shoulder or jumping whenever the phone rang. A part of her craved the sweet release of just giving up.

Maybe that would be easier than continuing this nightmare.

After all, he possessed so much more rage than she did.

He was surely going to win.

At that moment, a high-pitched whine began shrilling in her ears. As Steve moved closer, savoring his ability to intimidate her, she picked up her knife from the pan and turned back to face him. She stifled an insane urge to parody the stewardess's hallmark "Coffee, tea, or me?"

The whine in her ears became louder as she rose up on her toes, preparing to lunge at him with the knife.

Just then, a tiny, barely perceptible flicker appeared in Abby's peripheral vision. Steve seemed frozen in mid-stride. The tick-tock of her grandmother's clock slowed to a rhythmic boom, like the inexorable stomp of a giant. Abby glanced at the flicker, and could just make out a large, shimmering orb that glistened in the air like a child's soap bubble. It floated in and out of her field of vision, hovering near her elbow. She couldn't detect a face anywhere in the opalescence, but in her mind, she heard a clear, compelling voice.

"Stop! Wait! Think!"

In her murderous calm, Abby wryly appreciated the simplicity of it.

She stopped.

She waited.

She thought.

The shimmering bubble still hovered. Abby's knife clattered on the floor, and she assumed the fighting stance she had practiced in karate class. Steve faltered, surprised.

She looked him in the eye, and said in her lowest, quietest voice, "If you ever touch me again, I will put your balls into your throat."

They faced off, attacker and attacked, the roles slowly reversing. With a millimeter's shift in balance, he began to back down. He unclenched his fists, lowered his arms to his sides, turned away slightly, shook his head, and gave a nervous laugh.

"Damn, girl!" Then he pivoted on his heel, strode to the door, and slammed it hard as he left.

As Abby went limp and collapsed to the floor, she could have sworn the whine in her ears became a faint whinny, like a horse way off in the distance.

<hr />

Still wandering in the torn, crackling filaments of Abby's thoughts, I hear a voice calling out, "Grace! Wake up! Hell's bells, woman, you're The Baker!"

Like raindrops converging on a windowpane, all the remnant pieces of my awareness begin to gradually flow together. I blow the fuzz out of my thoughts, and try again to focus. To my astonishment, I sense a man riding past on a light colored stallion, dressed all in black, and he ... no it couldn't be ... yes it is.

He winks at me.

Through the cascade of images, I remember how I became locked into fear and despair, Abby's and my own. I throw all my energy into pulling myself together, find the resonance of Possibilities and just to be on the safe side, sing "The Sweet By and By," and begin falling, falling, until ...

... with profound relief, I land on the cool linoleum in my blessed kitchen, where Eureka ecstatically licks my face.

I settle into my favorite wooden rocker, pull him up on my lap and stroke his soft fur. An hour passes before I can stop shaking.

"I never understood how dangerous it can be to try and help people if you can't establish where you end and they begin. Also, it seems like my own grief and fear came right along with me, and it all got muddled up."

As memory returns, I feel sick and furious.

"The good news is that they caught that monster! They should tattoo a big skull and crossbones on his forehead so he never has the chance to hurt anyone again.

"And I think they're moving me to a better place.

"And I shouldn't be playing around with dissolving my thoughts into the thoughts of real people. It's dangerous. I got lost in Abby's thoughts and it all became mixed in with my own nightmare. I couldn't find myself and I couldn't make myself wake up. And in the end, I didn't help her, either."

Eureka pushes his cold nose into my hand and sighs. Then we both sigh together.

"There are some terrible people in the world. I know you know. But sometimes it's easy to forget, when things are just cruising along like Route 66. It's easy to forget that predators abound, and we have to be smart and defend ourselves, not just give up."

Can't help it. The tears are flowing like a fountain now.

"I kept trying to get free, but I was stuck in the honeycomb, just like a fly in a spider's web."

He sits up and barks and I pull his warm, little body close to me.

"You're right. I'm only going to dissolve my thoughts into those of people I already made. Real people are too unpredictable, their thoughts are too strong, and one set of real problems is enough. But I still wish I could figure out a way, because it seems like a possible means of communicating." I grab a Kleenex and blow my nose.

"And I HAVE to wake up, I really need to tell everyone that I'm OK now."

Then I realize what else is bothering me. "Eureka, who

do you suppose that guy was in the cowboy getup?"

He jumps down to fetch his favorite ball and sets it down on my feet.

"He saved me, Eureka, and helped Abby, too. Saved her life, when you get right down to it. He just came out of nowhere, and I have no idea if he's in Possibilities, or in the real world, or where exactly. But he did seem a little familiar, and I'm sure he's not anyone that I molded, sang, or otherwise baked up. I'm going to be on the lookout for him; seems like he might have some answers."

Chapter 7
Pennies from Heaven

1985

I have a scandalous idea. It comes to me while I'm fishing in the creek. Rather than just sampling the thoughts of people who are already in Possibilities, I could create dough people whose lives I want to try out.

Making up people for the express purpose of stowing away in their thoughts. That's just wrong.

My body may be kapuee, but my conscience is alive and well.

I resolve not to do it.

But then ... you know how we all make New Year's resolutions about losing weight, or volunteering more, or being more tolerant with our in-laws, and those resolutions just wither over time? Maybe from fatigue, or weakness of character, or resentment, or just plain willfulness?

Did I ever claim to be a saint? I always try to follow the Bible, you know that, but I'm human, and sometimes I give in to human temptations. Like that time when ... never mind.

Anyway, back to the dough people idea.

When you come right down to it, this is my dream, no

one else's. It's not as though any of this is real.

In truth I'm a harmless old lady in a nursing home bed. All this leisure time is suffocating me!

Or maybe I just have a contrary nature and unhealthy curiosity that seeks unconventional pastimes.

"Well, shoot!" I exclaim aloud, startling Eureka, who is snoozing in the grass. "I'm in an unconventional fix, right? The rules are a little different here, in case you hadn't noticed." He snorts.

Seems harmless enough. So long as I keep it to people I make here in Possibilities, I should be all right.

I think back through the list of people I always admired, and decide to start with Cyd Charisse, since it was a tune from one of her movies that got me started with this new pastime. I bake up my best replica of Cyd Charisse, put her on a stage in the town theater, wait until she's dancing, hum, vibrate, feel the gear slip, and whoosh, find my thoughts cozied in between hers.

What fun! What a shame I never learned to ballet dance in real life.

After the applause subsides, I slip away and rest on a park bench.

"It's like being an actress, and playing make believe," I tell Eureka, who spins in a circle chasing his own tail. "OK, no offense, but I am definitely not interested in tucking into your thoughts. But I would like to expand this activity into all kinds of things I never did in real life."

If I don't try them now, when will I ever get the chance?

Well, true confessions, this new enjoyment becomes a frequent activity over the next few … oh, heck, I don't know how long. Time just slips away from me here.

I try out all sorts of new identities. I dissolve into the thoughts of an auctioneer, a rodeo trick rider, and a pilot doing loop-de-loops in a little, yellow biplane.

How exhilarating! Heck! I could even try being a man. Do all the fun things the boys got to do that girls didn't.

At first it feels a little awkward trying to walk as a boy, kind of like trying to play the piano with an extra finger I imagine. *Now I know why men strut in that bowlegged way. Trying to avoid colliding with their privates.*

But I have great fun setting off contraband fireworks in the school lockers, spitting watermelon seeds at the mayor, swimming buck naked in the creek, guzzling beer and playing pool with the guys. As a finale, I pee my name, "Grace Gottlieb" into the snow in bright yellow.

Of course, it's only a matter of time until I realize I can experience romance from a whole new perspective, but the truth is, it's been decades since I thought about lovemaking. On the other hand, now that I'm young again, I'm starting to notice those long forgotten stirrings.

Would that be cheating on Hiram? I mean, he's dead, and I'm dreaming.

Well, I know this all sounds trite and trivial, but in my situation, would you be any different?

Pretty soon I'm ready for more challenge. But first I need more knowledge of the world. After all, like I told you earlier, I only made it through the sixth grade in school before I had to quit to help out at home when Mama died. The furthest I ever got from the Iowa Heartland was Chicago.

So I visit the Library and read up on all kinds of geography, history, and anthropology, and I start to learn all the different kinds of people and lifetimes I never knew about before. There are so many places to visit, so many things to encounter and try out, so many experiences to have!

All it takes is a little dough, and a little show!

I dissolve into the thoughts of a kid from the ghetto giving his college valedictorian speech, an opera diva perfecting her signature aria, and after that, a railroad tycoon wheeling and dealing. I "hitchhike" in the minds of a trapeze artist in the circus, a Parisian painter, and a South Pole explorer. I mold my image of the stunning Miss Lily Langtry and ride along on her touring train through the Wild West.

I confess, as Miss Lily I did have some very intriguing male companions. Did you know that she had a long and passionate affair with the Prince of Wales? But that's personal.

I even accompany a Sherpa climber on Mount Everest. Those people deserve more glory than they get, that's for sure.

The long and short of it is this: you can't have all those experiences without it changing you. Every place you go, every person you meet, every life you learn about, it enriches your own life. Every new sight brings new understanding, every new sound brings new awareness. Every new idea brings expanded thinking and creativity, and discriminating wisdom.

I had a wonderful life, no question. Rich in love and generosity and appreciation for the things that matter. But now I also see what I missed.

Nowadays, people are more worldly. They can watch movies, read books, use their cell phones and computers and the Internet, they can see videos on YouTube of all kinds of things!

But for me, with my background, trying out different kinds of lives, even just for a few moments, has been a *gobsmacking* revelation (I recently learned that word in Edinburgh).

I don't know what to make of Possibilities, but I surely am growing by leaps and bounds. And along with that, the tapestry of my old life is being replaced in my mind by a weaving of people, places and events of my own choosing, which is continually evolving into newfound motifs.

Still, exciting as all of that may be, when I lay my head down on the pillow at night, my thoughts inexorably return to my home and loved ones, especially when I hear their voices drift up from the well. Some of my favorite times are when Lily reads me letters from Iris. Makes me feel like I'm right there with her and my great-granddaughter in Detroit, more popularly known as Motown (short for what we used to call it, "Motor City").

⚜

August 21, 1983
Dear Grandma Grace:

Poppy is a now a 5-year-old scamp with a healthy irreverence for all things grownup and dull. She seems to have some kind of internal litmus test to decide the worth of things. If I had to put it into words, it would be something like, "is this either joyful or useful?" If yes, then she figures it has value, but if no, then she has no patience for it. When her kindergarten teacher rings the bell on a gorgeous late summer day to signal the end of recess, Poppy figures it's time to practice her cartwheels and somersaults.

Her antics frequently result in diplomatic notes from her teacher, written in neat longhand and decorated with little frowny face stickers. Poppy and I ceremoniously tear these notes to little pieces and flush them down the toilet.

Lily paused in her reading. "Mom?"

Grace slumbered on.

"Mom, it's a letter from Iris, she's writing to you about Poppy, remember Poppy? Your great-granddaughter? She inherited your beautiful hair, Mom, which makes Iris and me so envious — somehow we got Dad's boring brown hair instead. Course I fixed that with henna a long time ago!"

Lily watched her mother, wondering what thoughts Grace might be having, and if she was trying to speak. But Grace's shrunken form remained still and silent. Lily shook her head and leaned back in the wooden rocking chair they had moved from Grace's kitchen to her room at Elegant Manor.

"At least there's a little more space here to move around in," she said. She shifted her weight to get comfortable, and continued reading Iris's sprawling handwriting.

⚜

Laura looked up from her textbook. "What are you writing, Iris?"

"It's a letter to my grandmother."

"The one you told me about? Who's in the coma?"

"Uh-huh. I promised Mom I would write letters to her, and Mom reads them out loud, so they both get to hear them. Mom thinks Grandma can hear people talking, and I really hope that's true. But either way, at least it makes us feel better.

"Anyway, I've written about Poppy already. I'm not sure how to explain why I'm unemployed and in graduate school."

She continued typing.

Things were pretty meager for Poppy and me after her Dad left and got remarried. To make a long story short,

THE WELL

I left my job waitressing at Burt's Bophouse in Nebraska and, with the help of my brother Pete, entered graduate school in 1982.

Iris mulled over how to describe the situation to an 80-year-old woman who moved into her husband's family farmhouse at age 26, and never left. Until she became comatose.

I've been here for a year now, working on my doctorate in Clinical Psychology. Graduate school is kind of like redoing the bathroom tile. You get halfway into it before you realize how much work it is, but by then the bathroom is half torn apart and there's no choice but to finish the job. I've laid everything on the line here and there really is no turning back.

So I'm in what feels like a giant funnel (or, maybe more like a gaping abyss), and there is only a single exit, which becomes increasingly narrow, until I splat out the other end with my cap, gown and debts firmly in place.

We are all sleep-deprived. We slog through hours of coursework, run hundreds of subjects for our research projects, and see patients at the local mental health clinics. We economize either by living in groups, or in roach-infested rooms, on less than poverty wages, grubbing the thrift stores for professional clothes at miserly prices, subsisting on apples and popcorn, and wondering if we can meet the rent next month.

A comically grim situation, that's what graduate school really is. Besides all of that, I bet you think I must be plumb crazy to want to work with crazy people!

Iris stopped and reread. It sounded a little wordy, although Grace would understand the part about subsisting on apples and popcorn. She decided to describe Detroit itself, since Grace had never been there.

The pictures on the graduate program brochure looked so inviting! And there are some beautiful places here, with friendly people. And Detroit is very green in summer.

But the lush vegetation is thanks to wilting humidity, and the low cloud cover makes me feel a little stifled sometimes. Wish I could rest my eyes on the horizon of an Iowa cornfield.

The campus is smack in the middle of old brownstone neighborhoods made up of broad, littered streets and dilapidated homes whose bricks are sullied by time and grime. Many of them have been deserted; their burned and broken windows stare at us like empty eye sockets over lawns of scrub grass and weeds.

On the mile-long path from the campus to our jobs at the University Hospital complex, my friend Laura and I pass abandoned offices and storefronts with signs hanging catawampus and banging in the wind. Weedy wildflowers bloom in defiance of the shards of broken glass glittering on the cracked sidewalks. The wind is like an invisible giant that blasts the boulevards, sometimes nearly knocking us off our feet.

I bet in your day Detroit was a happenin' place! All that gorgeous Art Deco design and hot jazz!

Now I see a woefully neglected place brimming over with all this rich history. I hope that someday, someone goes to the time and expense to restore Detroit, but for now, I just want to finish graduate school and get back home.

Iris stopped to reflect how Grace was always so encouraging about whatever people did to expand themselves and make their lives better.

Please don't get the wrong idea, Grandma. You taught me there are blessings or lessons in any situation, and I have two friends here who are genuine beacons in the dark, named Laura and Cassidy.

Every now and then, we manage to get out for a foreign film at the Detroit Institute of Arts, or for breakfast and people watching at the Eastern Market, and Poppy loves going to Belle Isle for picnics. But for the most part, we just work, work, work.

I have read everything I can find in the Library about Detroit. I dress in a mink coat and high heels, and go strutting down my best replica of Grand Circle Park on my way to the Fox Theater's gala opening in Detroit on September 21, 1928.

It's a big production, complete with a silent film, a history of Detroit since 1701, and a competitive rendition of a Rockettes' type of dance company. This really is a "happenin'" place! But I'm a little worried about Iris. At least it sounds like she has some good friends.

⚡

Iris fixed dinner for her two friends and herself in the studio apartment she rented just north of Detroit, in a quiet suburb called Royal Oak. Although they had a full size bathtub, Iris and Poppy shared a pullout sofa bed for sleeping, and the galley kitchen was separated from their living/sleeping/eating space only by a narrow counter.

On the other hand, Iris liked that Poppy was attending school in Royal Oak rather than the inner city, and felt incredibly blessed to have a matronly neighbor who enjoyed babysitting her for a small cost, which Iris's brother Pete was helping to cover.

She served up peanut butter and bananas on raisin bread, with wine for the grownups. They heard a snap and squeak from the cupboard.

"Poppy, it's Showtime!" Iris called.

Poppy raced in, flung open the cupboard door and jumped aside as a little critter with a mousetrap attached to its tail flung itself onto the floor and raced to the living room.

Iris sighed in resignation. "Try to follow it, honey, we don't want it dying under the couch, it will start to smell really bad. But don't touch it!"

Laura and Cassidy smiled in commiseration. They also battled roaches and rodents.

Iris lowered her voice, "I don't know what to do about her school behavior."

"What is she doing?" Laura asked.

"It's more like what she's not doing. She just seems to operate on her own agenda, although when they formally test her letter and number knowledge, she's apparently at grade level, so I guess she's understanding the lessons. She just does things in her own time and her own way.

"They gave Poppy a test that measures how well you can pay attention for ten minutes. They told her to listen to a series of words on an audiotape and tap the table whenever she heard the word 'cat.' But after a few minutes, Poppy stopped working because, 'the man is just saying the same thing over and over.'

"So she technically failed the test. But the thing is, she's right! He does say the same thing over and over. She didn't see the point of doing it. Does that make her stupid or savvy? Seems like common sense to me."

"I'm not sure that common sense is a valuable commodity in school," Laura suggested. "As I recall, kindergarten is all about repetition and redundancy, all those letter and number drills. Come to think of it, I don't think that common sense is much appreciated in graduate school, either."

They all laughed at the painful truth of that as Iris reflected on her recent letter to Grace.

July 01, 1984

Happy Fourth of July! We plan to celebrate by going to the Freedom Festival; they shoot off fireworks over the Detroit River between the city and Canada on the other side. I'm really looking forward to the show.

I wanted to tell you a little more about my friend, Cassidy; she's the quintessential free spirit. I noticed her walking in front of me on the first day of orientation, a human gazelle with porcelain skin and strawberry blonde hair.

"She should be on a billboard modeling something," I thought to myself. Imagine my surprise when Cassidy strode right up the steps into the Psychology building, and straight into the meeting room where I was headed.

Feeling a little intimidated by the crowd of professors and other students, I followed her to the refreshments table, and watched, incredulous, as she selected orange juice and a powdered sugar donut. I wondered how the heck she was going to eat that donut without showering powdered sugar all down her front.

*I chose a much safer cake donut, and slid carefully
onto the seat next to her. Cassidy looked at me, and in
a voice reminiscent of Lauren Bacall at her most sultry,
commanded, "Now your job is to tell me if I have powdered
sugar on my moustache," thus forever endearing herself to
me.*

Cassidy was an iconoclast from start to finish. She could
grasp the most convoluted concepts in a flash, but to the
dismay of her friends, often amused herself by exploring
the run-down neighborhoods alone, on her bicycle, rum-
maging through abandoned homes, and "rescuing" vintage
items that caught her interest. She then furnished her room
with these questionable *objets d'art*.

Her "treasures" ranged from blatant kitsch, such as her
black velvet painting of a topless raven-haired temptress
("my Tahitian beauty"), to the utterly morbid, semi-decap-
itated doll painted with red blotches to depict bloodstains
("Life isn't always pretty.").

Her place resembled her mind – expansive, eclectic,
and willing to consider all things sacred or profane with
equally fierce honesty.

What Cassidy could not tolerate was the pedantic dron-
ing of arrogant professors. When a smug academician tried
to embarrass students by thrusting Rorschach inkblots in
their faces, demanding, "What do you *really* see?" Cassidy

slammed the table with her hand and loudly declared what they were all too embarrassed to admit: "I see genitalia in every one of those!"

Cassidy reminded Iris of Poppy in so many ways. When Poppy turned six, Laura and Cassidy helped to celebrate. Without hesitation, Poppy and Cassidy simultaneously reached for the glittery birthday cards and rubbed them on their faces.

November 03, 1984

> *Grandma Grace, how are you? I thought you might get a kick out of Poppy's latest misadventure. She was so excited I was mixing up a chocolate cake that she leaned in too close and her hair got caught up in the beater!*
>
> *Not sure what hurt more, her scalp or her pride. I had to get the scissors and give her a pixie cut right on the spot. She looks pretty cute with it, and we might just keep her hair short, at least for the rest of the summer.*
>
> *We have given our professors new names, because we found their old ones too boring. Our methodology professor is Dr. Statistics, our counseling teacher is Herr Healer, and we've named the most lecherous faculty member Professor Perv.*

Detroit seemed to be all about layers. There were layers of perma-dirt in the shabby brick rentals; layers of archival theory to wade through in the classes, and layers of poverty everywhere they looked.

Then there were the layers of deodorant and talcum needed for the steamy summers, or layers of clothing against the bitter cold in wintertime.

Three times each week for two years, Iris and Laura applied the appropriate layers and hurried to their jobs at the mental health center, then walked back to campus together.

"Apples really are the most amazing things," Laura said, admiring hers as she walked. "Crispy, tart, sweet, juicy, all at once — has there ever been anything to compare? And they fill you up, fight your cholesterol, clear your internal plumbing and your teeth, and they're cheap. There really is just nothing quite so terrific as an apple. No wonder Eve wanted to share this wonder food with her lover."

"I feel the same about almonds. I swear I could survive on them, although I doubt they would keep me regular the way apples do."

"Together they make a complete meal, though, don't you think?"

"Yes, with a little chocolate for dessert."

Iris stopped suddenly. "Ooh! A penny! Pick it up; we could use some luck!"

Laura bent down to retrieve the shiny copper disc from the cracked sidewalk and handed it to her. "Here, you take it. You have that statistics final exam tomorrow."

"Thanks, God knows I need luck to pass it."

Iris tucked the penny into the pocket of her down coat,

and headed over to the basement of Old Main, where the Psychology lab was housed.

Old Main's massive, yellow brick edifice was arguably the cornerstone of the University, brooding over the corner of Cass and Warren with sullen magnificence. Despite its long and venerable history, Old Main's interior more closely resembled a woebegone citadel than a proud landmark. Floors and ceilings had endured countless floods and leaks, paint was peeling from the walls, homeless residents made certain corners their own at night, and the basement stank of mold and urine. After dark, it was easy to imagine a haunting or two as the walls, weary of their century-long burden, creaked and groaned in protest.

For the umpteenth time, Iris took a deep breath and descended the stairs to the Lab, where she was testing 100 subjects for her research.

"It would be easier to entice Poppy to eat brussel sprouts than to round up undergraduates and entice them to brave these old hallways after dark," she told Laura earlier. Still, she only needed 20 more subjects, and could then start running the statistical analyses.

But Iris's progress was in jeopardy from something even more grim than Old Main's basement.

"To use a fractured analogy, I'm starting to see a light at the end of that funnel," she confided to Laura, "if only I can continue evading those squirrelly invitations from You Know Who."

Nearly every week after class, Professor Perv cornered her. "Come on over this weekend and party with us. We have a lot of fun."

Iris had already learned that the "fun" included plenty of legal and illegal refreshments, and often led to group gropes that were surreptitiously photographed for later leverage and coercion. She knew of other graduate students whose progress was delayed one year or more due to a jilted professor's caprice or malice. Sometimes, it resulted in their failure to graduate ... ever.

Coming up with excuses was becoming more and more challenging.

She shook the worries out of her head and set up her equipment. About one of every four subjects Iris scheduled to meet her at Old Main never arrived or called. She found herself waiting in vain for yet another no-show.

Geez! A wasted evening, no dinner, and class at 7:30 tomorrow morning.

She picked up a sleepy Poppy from the neighbor's house, and told her to take a quick bath. Poppy's look was full of reproach. As a guilt offering, Iris handed her the last fudgesicle from the freezer, and Poppy plodded away.

As she ran hot water over three days of dirty dishes, Iris wondered for the hundredth time how her daughter could crave fudgesicles in the middle of winter. A screech, followed by a wail, echoed from the bathroom. She rushed down the hall.

Poppy stood, staring helplessly at her fudgesicle floating in the toilet bowl, where it had splash-landed after a large moth startled her into flinging it through the air.

Iris regarded her woeful face. "Sorry, honey, that was the last one."

Poppy crumpled to the floor and burst into tears. This was so uncharacteristic, and Iris was so exhausted and emotionally spent herself, that she slid down the wall and joined her. They sat huddled together on the cold linoleum until Poppy declared, "I hate this place! Let's leave, Mama! I miss the farm and the diner and everybody that loves us."

Iris wondered if Poppy had been reading her mind. A six-year-old clairvoyant? "Poppy, you know that we're doing all this so we can have a better life."

"What was wrong with our old life?"

"Baby, I couldn't pay the bills. I had to borrow money from your Uncle Pete. This way we have a future, and ..."

Iris stopped. Despite Poppy's childlike wisdom, logic was useless. She didn't yet understand how heartless the world could be.

A diversion tactic, instead. "Guess what Laura and I found today? A lucky penny! Would you like to keep it?" She fished the penny out of her pocket and held it up to the light.

"OK." A small voice, and no hand reaching out.

Iris held her close and stroked her hair. Poppy sighed deeply and snuggled in. "Time for the Sandman?"

"OK."

They got up off the floor, opened the sleeper couch, and laid down. After dozing for an hour or so, Iris returned to the kitchen to confront the dishes.

February 20, 1985

Grandma Grace, I wish I could talk to you. I'm starting to think that coming to graduate school was a really bad mistake. I am taking four classes, working part time for a pittance, camping out in a virtual dungeon waiting for subjects who no-show, trying to avoid the clutches of smarmy professors, and I have barely enough money to survive.

I have no time for sleep, or playing with Poppy, much less daily chores or grocery shopping. Poppy is having trouble at school, the weather sucks, and I miss home so much. I've been thinking maybe it's time to cut my losses and give up this idea of being a Psychologist. What was I thinking?

Hearing Iris's letter, I'm more worried than ever.

"Sounds like she's pretty downhearted and thinking about dropping out of school," I tell Eureka. "That's just wrong! Iris will make a fine Psychologist, she really cares about things, she knows how to listen to people, and she always has good suggestions. Shoot! She's perfect for that kind of work. I wonder how I can communicate with her.

Nobody hears me through this dang well. And I'm not so crazy about trying to hum my way into real people's thoughts after what happened with Abby."

I know that the snowy world only has two exits – one into my useless body, the other into Possibilities.

But maybe...

"This well has to lead somewhere. It has a top, so it has to have a bottom. Or maybe it's just a plain old wishing well." I reach into my pocket and pull out an old penny, dropping it in. "I wish I could find a way to help her."

The penny disappears. I wonder if my wish is canceled out.

"Maybe I should drop down something that I can hold onto."

I run into the kitchen and return with a ball of yarn. I lean over the side of the well again, and start unrolling the yarn. To my disgust, it disappears right at the water's level, and when I try to roll it back up, it's just gone. As before with the rocks, there is neither a reflection nor a whisper on the water's surface to show where the yarn went.

"There must be a way!" I insist to Eureka, who growls and gnaws on his bone. "You really do have a dog's life. I wonder if you think you're in a dream, too."

Hey! A dream! What if I enter Iris's dream and try to give her a message? Maybe that would be safer than when she's awake and her mind is fully active. I could get in, talk to her, and get out without becoming stuck like I did with Abby.

With new hope, I focus on Iris, ensure that she's asleep, hum, vibrate, feel the now familiar slip of a gear, and dissolve into her dream images, then begin trying to create an image of my own.

But Iris's dream doesn't make any more sense than most dreams do. There's a bespectacled little guy who keeps stroking his beard saying, "hmm," a naked lady on a couch with long blonde hair, and a girl in ruby slippers who is clicking her heels together and repeating, "There's no place like home, there's no place like home."

Honestly, I can't even get a word in.

Finally I focus on a white horse that canters by, and imagine a pink tulle ball gown.

Maybe she'll notice me like this.

"Iris! This isn't the time to quit! Don't let your dreams die!"

⚒⚒⚒

Laura and Iris crunched through the heavy snow on their way to the mental health clinic. Iris yawned loudly.

Laura smiled at her.

"I swear, Laura, every time I started to doze off last night, I had the oddest dreams. Finally I just got up and worked on a statistics assignment and woke up this morning stretched out over the table with my books and papers all around me. And the last dream just stayed with me."

"Hmm. I'm a shrink, you know. I'll analyze it for you."

"Aside from just chalking it up to indigestion? OK, I'll try, but it's pretty mixed up. There was my grandmother, but she was decked out like Lady Godiva, riding nude through Coventry on a snow white steed to protest the oppression of the common folk.

"Then she morphed into Glinda the Good Witch from the 'Wizard of Oz,' and I guess I was Dorothy. No, wait. I was the scarecrow. And I was running around insisting that I need a brain, and grandmother-Glinda held her wand over me, and in her twinkly Billie Burke voice told me to click my heels together three times and keep repeating, 'I already have a brain. I already have a brain.' And something about dyeing, I guess like dyeing clothes?"

Laura laughed out loud.

"OK, Ms. Freud, so what do you make of it?"

"Um, she wants you to ride through Detroit naked on a snow white steed, follow the yellow brick road and tie-dye your shirts?"

"Cute."

"It sounds like either your grandmother, or you, if it's your subconscious, is reassuring you that you're smart, Scarecrow!"

"But was she telling me I already have a brain, so I don't need a doctorate to prove it? Or did she mean that I already have a brain, so I should apply it and get through graduate school?"

"An ambiguous dream. What a rarity. They're usually

clear as mud."

"So you don't know what to make of it, either."

"I'm a highly biased friend who wants you to finish graduate school with me. What really matters is what do *you* make of it?"

For the next few days, Iris thought about the dream and her grandmother, lying prone and unresponsive, not giving up even in the face of death.

Grandma never quit anything in her life, she thought. *Not when her mama died young and she raised her siblings, not after she had three miscarriages, not when they were a few dollars away from losing the farm, not ever.*

Grace believed in regrouping, not retreating; she acknowledged setbacks, but never defeats.

The more Iris thought about it, the more certain she felt that Grace would want her to finish graduate school. *Or maybe my subconscious wants me to finish graduate school. Actually, I really want to finish graduate school!*

The next day, Iris shared her thinking with Laura, who danced a little jig, and then more seriously prompted her. "And what are you going to do about Professor Perv?"

"I don't know. He could really sabotage me."

"Hey look! Another penny."

The next day they found two more.

Laura shook her head. "How odd to keep finding these shiny, new pennies amidst all this urban blight."

"I sure hope they work. I have to meet with Dr. Statistics

tomorrow and I just want him to sign off on my data so that Professor Perv can't require me to run more subjects."

"Here, just for luck, take both pennies." She tucked them into Iris's pocket.

"Thanks! I feel so well armed now."

It was several months before Iris found the time to write again.

May 7, 1985

Great news! My data was approved, and I'm on the home stretch of completing my dissertation. It helped that Professor Perv got arrested for indecent exposure over by Rouge Park! Seriously. And the story gets even better. Word has it that he was busted by a Detroit mounted police officer. Kinda fitting for such a horse's a..., don't you think?

Anyway, the upshot of all that uproar was that I was assigned another prof to take his place on my dissertation committee, and the new guy is very reasonable. Over the past few months, Laura, Cassidy and I have continued to progress with our work, studies and research, and we're beginning to see the end of that funnel after all.

Poppy, meanwhile, has made a satisfactory peace with her kindergarten teacher.

Oh, and here's the funniest part! The other day, I walked from class to work with Cassidy instead of Laura. As we walked, Cassidy reached into her pocket, pulled out a handful of pennies, and scattered them on the sidewalk. When I asked what she was doing, she said, "Oh, I just feel sorry for people who live around here, so many of them are the working poor, families with no medical insurance for when their kids get sick, and I don't have enough money to help them, so I throw pennies on the ground.

"Dumb, I know, but I figure someone might find them and feel lucky, maybe a little more optimistic, and that will help them keep going until they get a real break."

That's right. My zany, wonderful friend has been secretly throwing "lucky" pennies on the ground, and unbeknownst to her, my other wonderful friend and I have been picking them up.

Seated on the edge of the well, I watch the last red finger of setting sun relinquish its hold on the horizon. The evening air is sweet with moist hay, while the crickets and fireflies hail and twinkle their Good-Evenings. I call half-heartedly into the well, even as I know my words will be unheard: "Well, Lily, our girl has learned that hope costs next to nothing, but its effects are priceless."

Oh, how I miss them, my dear ones. I pick up Eureka and hug his warm softness close to me.

"Well, the dream communication didn't go so well, and I'm still locked out of my body. Or locked in, however you think about it. The thought of never being able to see them all again just claws at me. And even though this has been great fun, none of it is real, and I just want to go home!" He licks my tears and cuddles into my arms as I follow the trail of light from the kitchen window across the grass to the back screen door.

Chapter 8

Road Trip Down Memory Lane

1986

The automatic doors at Elegant Manor swept open, and the blast of air conditioning gave Lily goose bumps. She wrinkled her nose at the familiar dueling smells of overcooked broccoli and industrial strength cleanser, then sniffed at her sleeve and frowned.

All my clothes are starting to smell like this place.

The black and white tile gleamed in the last rays of sunlight as she made her way past the staff lounge and down the hall. She wondered for the hundredth time why the nurses' shift change took place just before dinner, when residents were hungry and the dining room staff was trying to set up.

At their station, nurses were in a flurry writing or reading the daily notes in residents' charts. They rushed down the halls to round up their charges and wheel them into the dining room. A few of them nodded and smiled at her, with "Hi, Mrs. Olsen, how are you?" and "She's been peaceful today, Mrs. Olsen," and "Would you like us to send in a dinner tray for you?"

Lily responded with obligatory smiles and chat, and was relieved to abandon the cheerful pretense as she entered Grace's room. She set her purse down on the little nightstand, then picked up the phone and called home. "Hey, babe. How was your day?"

"Not bad." Mitch's deep voice calmed her nerves, as always. "Leonard came in for a tractor loan, the Murrays paid off their second, and there's a new couple buying the old Persinger place. Leonard was good to go, of course, and I'm pretty sure the new folks' references will check out."

"Sounds like high times," she teased, and he laughed.

"Makes the day go faster when there's work to do."

"Do you recall that I'm having dinner with Mom tonight?"

"Yeah, that's fine. Take as much time as you need, baby. I'll leave your pillow and blanket on the couch."

She laughed along with the smile in his voice. For almost thirty years, they had warned each other that whoever stayed out too late would have to sleep on the couch. So far, it had never happened.

"I'll be home around 8:00, I think. There's lasagna in the freezer, just reheat it at 350 for about twenty minutes, OK?"

"Got it."

Of course he's got it. He's become a real whiz at reheating frozen dinners.

"Thank you for understanding. I love you."

"Love you, too; see you later."

She smacked a kiss into the receiver, and hung up.

She thought of writing a cookbook for women with family members in a nursing home. She'd become a real expert at cooking a whole week's worth of dinners on Sunday, so they could be reheated and enjoyed by a husband whose only dinner companion was the disgustingly pert, fresh-faced blonde on the 6:00 news.

Lily scanned the room to make sure things were in order, and noticed with pleasure that the African violets she'd brought in last month were blooming, in stark contrast to the quiet dormancy of the room and its occupant. Feeling the need for dark and privacy, she closed the door and the curtains, and sat down to rock in Grace's old chair. She regarded her mother's peaceful face, and wondered yet again how her hair managed to stay its dark color, not even salt and pepper, despite her advanced years and failing health.

She took Grace's limp hand in her own.

"Please, Mom," she said softly. "Please wake up. I just miss you so much. There's a big empty hole in the center of our lives where you used to be. There's so many things I want to talk with you about, and so many things I want to do with you that we never had a chance.

"We were so busy with things that didn't even matter, what were we thinking? Didn't we know we were on borrowed time?" Her voice quavered.

"Remember we talked about going on that Mississippi

river boat cruise? And maybe even taking a flight somewhere? We could go to New York and see the Statue of
Liberty! We can still do those things, it's not too late."

She lapsed into quiet tears, allowing herself the rare
luxury of grieving in solitude.

After a time, she blew her nose, then opened her purse
and pulled out a letter from Iris. She read to herself for a
moment, and then exclaimed, "Oh, Mama, I'm so proud
of Iris! She's about to be awarded her doctorate! I never
would have believed that my sassy, little scamp would become a Doctor of Psychology.

"We plan to celebrate with a road trip. Her girlfriend
offered to watch Poppy in Detroit while Iris flies over to
Des Moines, where I'll pick her up. She and I are going
down to Chicago to celebrate her graduation, and we'll
make a side trip to visit Inez and her family. You remember
Inez? Abel's younger sister? She used to come picnic with
all of us, over at The Shack behind the park, when she was
still a kid. Gee, I sure wish you were awake and could come
with us."

Lily's voice trailed off.

❧❖❦

It's cold. I pull my coat a little tighter and shield my
eyes to watch the geese fly south over skeletal trees that
shiver in the wind. From the well, I hear Lily begging me
to wake up, which just shreds my heart and soul. It sounds

like she's crying, and I begin to cry with her.

Doesn't she know I would wake up if I could?

Then she begins running on about Inez.

Of course I remember her, a mousey little thing who married that ne'er-do-well and had a passel of kids they couldn't afford to feed. Lucky for them Abel was so generous.

"I wish I could come with you, too," I call down the well, feeling pretty sorry for myself. It doesn't help my mood that the weather has turned frigid, and the vegetable garden is nothing but frosty, brown stubble. Even though I didn't "wish" it, Possibilities seems to be headed into winter, even though the way Lily was talking, it must be summer in the real world.

My winter, her summer, my coma, her life. Maybe we're stuck in a bad joke like permanent Opposite Day — ha ha.

Despite my best efforts, I am sinking into downheartedness, and maybe that's why my thoughts keep percolating with a notion I've had for a while — baking up a version of Hiram when he was young and handsome.

There are a host of things to consider before taking such a giant step. First, I still feel a little squeamish about baking up copies of family members. Even if they are already dead and buried, it feels kind of like trespassing on their immortal memory or something.

But beyond that, the truth is, well, I also have some mixed feelings about Hiram being around all the time.

Sure, it might help ease my homesickness, but I've grown pretty fond of being my own boss here. Men just always seem to assume they're in charge, and if you challenge them, they either get their back up and dig their heels in, or sulk and pout like little kids.

Still, there's no denying that I am lonesome for male company.

I mean, you know what it's like. All those pesky urges! I tell Eureka, "You can't expect a young woman not to have needs. Even if I don't really have a body, so to speak, the creative juices are flowing, and after all, he and I were married for half a lifetime."

Then come the wearisome debates with my conscience. *You can't just bake up family members for your own selfish needs. It feels wrong.*

"Oh beans! Didn't I bake up all the people in Possibilities because I was lonely, and how is that different?"

Well, it just is, that's all. You don't really miss him, you just miss making whoopee with him.

"That's not true. Hiram was my best friend, my companion for most of my life, even if he was highly opinionated."

The bossiness question does give me pause. Time after time over the years, I had to work the way I communicated so that Hiram thought things were his idea. I remember when I really, really, really wanted one of those newfangled spin washers to replace my old wringer washer in the basement. It took weeks of carefully timed, subtle hints ("Oh, sorry, honey, don't mean to startle you with my cold hands, it's just so chilly down in the basement when I do laundry," and "Man, that danged ole washer just doesn't get your shirts as clean as I like 'em, does it?"). I kept leaving the Sears catalog open in the bathroom. I chatted up Mrs. Hansen on the phone while he sat at the kitchen table, telling her all about how I spent so much time doing laundry, it was really cutting into my pie-baking afternoons.

I just about split a gut laughing when Hiram declared, "You know, Grace, I think maybe we need one of those new spin washers." As though he came up with the idea himself.

Really, it was kind of ridiculous how I had to finagle just to keep him from thinking that I had ideas of my own.

After all, I managed the entire household and the kids without much in the way of help from him.

The last thing I want here and now is for Hiram to take shape in my dream world and start acting like he's running things.

But finally, loneliness and youthful urges win out. I shape up my dough, sing about love, and presto! He appears in a soft, white T-shirt that smells of soap and healthy sweat, and showcases his broad shoulders and muscular arms, his hard thighs and other parts threatening to burst through the worn blue jeans. A jolt of excitement zips through me.

⚜

Iris fiddled with the car radio and then turned it off. "Geez, I forgot that it's nothing but talk shows or static out here. How much farther? I'm getting hungry."

"We're almost there. I thought you said you brought some snacks with you."

"Yeah, but I'm craving a real meal. Besides, I have to pee, and it seems like the air conditioner isn't working so great. I stink!"

"It's summer in Illinois. Everybody stinks. There's not a deodorant made that can handle this weather. And don't tell me it's any better in Detroit." Lily lifted her hand and pretended to cringe at her underarm, then grinned at her daughter. "I hope that getting a doctorate hasn't made you hoity-toity."

Iris sighed and pulled out the thermos of ice water. "Tell me again why we're visiting these people that I barely remember and probably didn't like in the first place?"

"Partly just to have an excuse for a road trip with you. But also out of respect for your great-uncle Abel. He was married to my aunt Camelia, Mom's sister. You know he got kind of famous because of his amusement park, roller skating rink, furniture store, and all of that. Don't you remember going down there for family reunions and stuff? Well, Inez is Abel's youngest sister, which makes her Mom's youngest sister-in-law, and you did meet her at Abel's funeral a few years back. How can you not remember her and her kids? She has five!"

In her mind's eye, Iris conjured up blurry memories of a bunch of barefoot kids fighting over the porch swing at The Shack behind Abel's Place.

"Mostly I remember Aurora yelling that she was the boss of the yellow horse on the merry-go-round. And getting hit in the head by a toy boomerang that kept coming back. And a surprise food fight attack with mashed potatoes and gravy that ruined my new Christmas dress. And an assembly line of bald, squalling babies needing diaper changes. Yeah, Mom, those were the good old days," Iris rolled her eyes.

Lily made an abrupt right turn. "Here it is. Water Street."

Iris looked around. Water Street was a blast from the past, all right. Majestic oaks and maples cloaked the lane in dappled shade, while darkened brick homes peeked out like forgotten, distant relatives. Lily peered at the numbers on the curb.

"So ... anyway ... let me think. My mother Grace is the sister of Abels' wife, Camelia, so their kids are my cousins, which makes Abel's sister Inez's kids my second cousins. Meanwhile, you're my daughter, so that would make Inez's kids your second cousins, once removed, because of the generation difference." She shook her head and laughed. "So you and I are related to Inez through Grace's brother-in-law, see?"

"Stop, you're giving me a headache."

"Me, too! I don't know, Iris, the main point is that we all used to have fun over at Abel's Place when he was still alive, and we haven't seen these people for a long time. Oh, look, there's the house."

Iris stared in disappointment. This end of Water Street was locally known as the wrong side of the tracks. The three-story clapboard home obviously had good bones, but had been allowed to decline from proud to embarrassed.

Iris regarded the barefoot ragamuffins and empty beer bottles lined up along the steps and railings of the broad front porch. *How many of these kids actually live here?* she wondered.

Lily had given her the some of the Willard family history during the five-hour drive. Inez Willard had come from the same bare roots as her brother, Iris's great-uncle Abel MacGregor. She grew up in a sparsely appointed but loving farm home in Nebraska, where she was the much adored baby sister who arrived unexpectedly late in her parents' lives. Her father, a Scottish preacher, considered her a true gift from God, and treated her as such.

"But you know, that kind of unquestioning, unconditional adoration can lead a person to be naïve and easily fooled. Inez never developed the savvy she needed for seeing through a smooth-talking tenth grader named Doyle Willard. When she was barely fourteen years old, she and Doyle ran off to get hitched. It was a big mistake." Lily shook her head.

"Starry-eyed over his promises of big ventures and an exciting life, Inez soon found herself sinking into poverty, and she took in washing while they eked by on what he made from odd jobs.

Lily continued as she parked the car, "If it weren't for Abel doing so well for himself in Nebraska, and having a big heart, these folks might've just starved. Aunt Camelia used to complain about Abel sending Inez a monthly stipend, which continued as a trust fund after he died. And in fact, Abel didn't care much for Doyle and seldom visited them. But he had a soft spot for his baby sister, and couldn't let Inez and his nieces and nephews do without the necessities. Based on what we're seeing, I imagine that extra money is what stood between them and being homeless."

"Mom, how about if we just visit for a little while, and then go out to dinner at Stagecoach Sadie's? I saw one on the way into town."

Looking around at the house's weary façade and littered yard, Lily nodded. She stepped from the car to greet a haggard looking woman with a broad smile who stood on the front porch. "Hey, Inez!"

"Oh, look at you! My land, it's ages since I saw you, and look at Iris, all grown up!" She gave them smothering hugs, shooed children off the porch stairs, and gestured for them to sit down. "It's cooler out here than in the house." She called out to one of the girls, "Fern! Be a love and bring us out something cold to drink."

"But Mama! I'm fixin' to go look for that ghost that Cecil saw."

Inez scowled at her, "Fern, first of all, there's no such

thing as ghosts, and if there were, you couldn't see them in the daytime, and anyway, Cecil isn't sure what he saw."

"He is, too! I heard him talking to Mona about it."

"Fern, I need you to please go bring us some cold drinks, now go on!"

The girl tsk'ed loudly and slammed the screen door as she went into the house.

Lily smiled. "Don't they just have the wildest imaginations? What ghost is she talking about?"

"Well, let me back up a little, and I'll tell you what I know, but I'm sure I didn't get the whole story. Cecil is steady as a compass, but once you throw in Shelley, and then Mona, well, who knows what really happened?"

⋆⋆❖⋆⋆

Cecil Willard was the heartthrob of the neighborhood girls, but he only had eyes for Shelley. She was a blue-eyed blonde with budding curves and movements rapidly smoothing from gangly to graceful. In the privacy of her own room, decorated with posters of Disney characters and rock stars, she would scoop her stuffed animals onto the floor and indulge her fantasies of muscle bound heroes from the covers of dime store romance novels. Each imaginary vignette featured a desperately passionate abduction to the man's castle, or cave, depending on the story line, where he would satisfy both of their base urges, and then be too overcome by her beauty to live without her.

Caught between teddy bears and hormones, Shelley's self-image went through a major metamorphosis every hour, for better or worse.

Despite its hardscrabble appearance, the neighborhood's porches, alleys, and trees large enough for tree houses made Water Street a mecca for kids. In the winter, they hauled their wooden sleds over to the golf course's snowy hills, taking ride after ride until hunger or sheer exhaustion sent them home in search of hot chocolate with marshmallows.

On warmer, rainy days they gathered on someone's front porch and entertained themselves for hours, digging through boxes of comic books while curled up in smelly, woolen Army blankets.

But best of all were the summers. With so many large families, it was easy to pull together a block-wide game of Ditch'em that started right after breakfast and continued until angry parents summoned them "for the last time" to come inside or get locked out for the night.

Ditch'em was, hands down, their favorite pastime. The kids split into two teams, members of one team counting to 100 while the others found hiding places. Then the counting team looked for the hiding team.

"We all operate solo," Cecil reminded the players, something he often had to do because of the younger children in the game.

"No pairing up. When the counting team finds one of

the hiding team's guys, they tag him and that means he's now on the counting team, see? BUT! If the hiding team guy tags the counting team guy first, then he's on the hiding team.

"So the object is to get everybody on one team or the other, and then that team wins. If we have to go in for dinner before that happens, whichever team has the most kids wins. Got it?"

They gave Cecil understanding nods. He was taller than the others, his body hurrying into adolescence and constantly outgrowing his pant legs and shirtsleeves. His mop of curly hair topped a dirty face; a worry line already formed between the brows of his serious eyes. He had the sinewy strength of an alley cat. No one ever challenged his unspoken command of the group.

"Are there boundaries?" asked Mary, a ten-year-old new to the neighborhood.

"You can hide anywhere on the block," Cecil told her, "either side of the alley, any of the corner lots, all of it. Just remember you can't hide with someone else; you are operating on your own. Anyone caught cheating has to go home and take a bath."

They all groaned.

Cecil started pointing to each child as he counted off, "1, 2, 1, 2, 1, 2, 1, 2…" and then declared the 1's to be the counters, and told the 2's to "get going and hide!" Four children covered their eyes and began to count to 100, and four others took off at top speed, knowing full well that none of the counters could get all the way to 100. They might even stop counting at 30.

The game continued for hours. Each time a child was tagged by an opposing team member, he or she changed sides. One never knew for sure who was on which team, which made approaching each other a prickly challenge. They had never reached a point where every child was on the same team; it always came down to a majority. Cecil had an innate sense of fair play, and he moved kids in and out of groups, so that the same kids didn't win every day.

Shelley noticed how he always stood up for the underdog. Like the time she was walking home from school and found Cecil waging a furious defense of a smaller child against a gaggle of kids throwing snowballs made with rocks inside. He walked into the situation unknowingly, and was so outraged at the injustice that he hunkered down with the crying child and started hurling icy missiles at the bullies. Without thinking, Shelley joined him; they sent the attackers running home to their mothers.

"Why would they do something so unfair?" she wailed to Cecil. "What's the point of that?"

"Some folks make themselves feel bigger by picking on the weak." A frown creased his face. "I don't get it, but maybe it's 'cause they feel so crummy about themselves that they have to hurt other people to feel better."

After he walked Shelley home, Cecil bragged to her

mother about how brave she was.

Then came the time that she got hurt. While guarding first base in their empty lot softball game, she was knocked in the forehead by a hard, fast line drive. One moment she was hunched over, clutching her mitt and yelling at the pitcher; the next, she was on her back, opening her eyes to the sight of Cecil hovering over her, his worry line deeper than usual, his voice calling her name. There were little sparkly dots floating in her field of vision, a rushing sound in her ears, and nausea in her stomach. She tried to speak, but nothing came out.

"Shelley! Are you OK? You got knocked out by the ball. Mary went to get your mom. Just lie still, don't move, help is coming."

She closed her eyes and moaned, wishing that the world would stop spinning. A cool hand stroked her hair. She heard Cecil's voice continuing to reassure her: "Help is coming, Shelley, you're going to be fine, we're all here with you."

She lifted her head and spewed vomit all over him before passing out again. She awoke in her own bed, with the doctor and her mom murmuring quietly at the door. "... probably a mild concussion, just keep an eye on her pupils and call me if you see any change."

Cecil came by later that day with a chocolate bar, the sight of which made her feel queasy again, but she smiled and thanked him. She knew he had probably taken the risk of shoplifting it for her.

"You're not going to puke on me again, are you?" Cecil teased when she joined the group for Ditch'em a week later. She scrunched her face at him, and made an effort to avoid him the rest of the day. But she really couldn't stay away from Cecil for very long.

In our replicated farmhouse bedroom, Hiram and I regard each other with awkward familiarity. I wonder if he will have the awareness to be confused, finding himself a young man again, at home with me. I move near and hold his face in my hands. "Do you know how glad I am to see you?"

He scoffs, smiling, "Why, sweetness, you see me all the time!" He wraps his arms around my waist, tightens his hold, leans me backwards, and kisses me. Then he picks me up and carries me to the bed, covering my body with his as we sink into the down comforter.

Chapter 9

Solomon Sings and Abel Tips His Hat

"Who is this that appears like the dawn, fair as the moon, bright as the sun, majestic as the stars in procession?"

— *Song of Solomon, 6:9-10.*

It is achingly joyful for Hiram and I, just like the first time. Sweet and urgent all at once. Now I remember how I had loved him for so many years, how it started with this and then inched forward into children and work and grand-children and more work... but always, through thick and thin, the love. I catch my breath and turn to him again.

⋘❖⋙

Looking up from the porch, Inez abruptly went quiet as a raven-haired teen Jezebel in a full-skirted red dress strutted up the sidewalk. She needn't have bothered. Cecil's older sister, Mona, had known about the budding romance between Cecil and Shelley months ago. Mona was a natural born sleuth.

But she was more notorious for her looks. Iris would have sworn that Elizabeth Taylor was standing in front of them. In addition to the impossibly tiny waist and full hips, her lips and nails shone with bright crimson (*Is that "Cherries in the Snow?"* Iris mused. *Haven't seen that shade of red since I was a kid),* and her shiny gold ankle bracelet hinted at Cleopatra on her barge.

Indeed, Mona's favorite pastime was to settle on the top porch step with all the sinuous grace of a Nile queen, then lean back and watch the world through drowsy eyelids as if it were all just so boring.

With her thick black hair, smoldering hazel eyes and porcelain skin, Mona made most girls, and women for that matter, feel dowdy and askew.

Neighborhood gossip held that Mona was a tramp. She did nothing to slow the gossip, priding herself on being able to make men of all ages lose their ability to form complete sentences.

But she wasn't stupid. Keenly aware of her family's limited prospects, Mona made it her business to know anything and everything that happened in the neighborhood.

She knew, for example, that Mr. Simmons was a little too fond of the babysitter, that the babysitter's mom was a closet alcoholic, and that the frumpy woman up the block was caring for a brother perennially sick with some kind of disabling condition.

She knew that the unassuming owners of the house on the corner had inherited some money, closed up the place and left for a year-long cruise.

She knew that the milkman had a criminal record, and that the Librarian liked to dress up in harem clothes and belly dance behind her closed living room curtains.

But Mona also knew that the power behind having information is knowing when to use it. She kept her factoids to herself until such time as she might need to pull them out and play them like an ace in the hole.

Unlike Shelley, Mona knew exactly who she was at every moment, and she liked herself just fine. What she didn't like was her budget.

Mona needed spending money. Seeing a Help Wanted sign in the Library window, she put on a plain white blouse and long skirt, and went over to apply. She stood in line behind the frumpy woman with the sick brother, who was arguing with the Librarian.

"I returned those books! Your record keeping must be wrong!"

"I'll go check again, Vera, just wait here one minute." The Librarian sighed and disappeared to the back office. Mona impatiently tapped her foot and snapped her gum.

The woman turned to her, annoyed. "Do you mind?"

Mona reached into her mouth and slowly stretched a bit of gum into a long, pink string that extended almost to Vera's nose, then spiraled it back around her tongue. Vera gaped at her in disgusted fascination.

The Librarian returned. "Vera, we don't have those books. I'm sorry, but rules are rules. I can't renew your

Library card until you return the books that are missing. We've checked all over our shelves, and they're not here. Are you sure you've searched everywhere at home? What about in your car?"

The woman shook her head and sputtered, "I don't have them! This isn't fair!"

"Please understand, I just can't check out anymore books to you until you bring those back. I'm very sorry."

Vera spun around and nearly ploughed into Mona as she stormed out.

Mona smiled at the Librarian, trying to look studious. "I'm here to apply for the job, the one posted in the window."

The Librarian regarded Mona over a pair of bifocals. "How old are you?"

Rats! How old do I need to be to put books on a shelf?

She smiled. "Fifteen."

"Well, I'm sorry, dear, you have to be at least sixteen years old to be employed here."

"Damn!" Mona swore in a loud whisper. The Librarian smugly shook her head.

Mona popped her gum, then turned slowly and sashayed out of the Library as she sang aloud, "There's a place in France where the ladies wear no pants," to the tune of the popular harem dance song. She looked back to see the Librarian blushing bright red. But that was a small victory in the context of a larger defeat. She really needed to find a job.

Meanwhile, Shelley found herself cornered by an opposite team member in a day-long game of Ditch'em. Her only possible escape was to the empty house across the alley. She had heard Mona comment that the owners were gone on a cruise. She ran over and tried the door, feeling like a burglar. Locked, of course. She ran around the house, desperately seeking a bush or tree trunk large enough to hide behind.

That's when she saw the basement window, wedged open with a 2x4 block of wood.

She pulled the window open wider and slipped her legs through, until her foot landed on a solid surface. She planted both feet and slid into the basement.

She was standing on an old wooden kitchen chair that had been placed strategically underneath the window. *That's pretty handy*, she thought. The basement was dark and cool, smelling faintly of mildew and laundry detergent.

She reached up to pull the window closed behind her, only to find herself looking right into Cecil's reproachful face.

"Shelley! You can't go in there!"

She stopped, holding the window open while she poked her head out. "There's nobody here, Cecil, it's a perfect hiding place."

No sense trying to evade him now that he'd seen her. Better to tag him first so he had to change sides to her team.

As he knelt down in the grass, she rapped her hand on his and called out in victory, "I tagged you and you're on the number 1's team now! Ha!"

Cecil shook his head. "It's against the rules to break and enter into somebody's house," he declared with quiet certainty.

"Since when? You never said anything about that in the rules before."

A quizzical expression crossed his face. "Well, it's not like it ever came up before, Shelley, but anyone with any sense would know it."

She flushed with embarrassment at his implied meaning; that she had no sense.

"Nobody's been here for months. You know these folks are gone. I'm not hurting anybody. Besides, the window was already propped open, and this chair was already here. I didn't break anything." Her voice trailed off. She could hardly bear to be chastised by her secret flame.

Cecil sighed. "OK, but the tag doesn't count. You can't hide in people's houses, no matter if they're empty or not. It's a new rule."

Shelley sat down on the floor, humiliated and disconsolate. "Who cares?" she cried.

"Come out of there, c'mon, let's play; I'll give you a head start, OK?"

No response.

Cecil hesitated. It didn't feel safe leaving her here, but

how could he coax her to come out?

"Do you want me to come in and sit with you?"

Again, no response.

"OK, Shelley, I'm coming in. I didn't mean to piss you off."

Cecil climbed into the basement and sat down next to her, but Shelley didn't want him to see her crying. She jumped up. "Let's explore, since we're in here anyway."

"No, we're trespassing, sure as I breathe, and I don't want to get in trouble. Let's go!"

But Shelley turned and bolted up the stairs, towards the thin line of light coming from underneath the door. She turned the doorknob and found herself in a bright, cheery kitchen, empty of furnishings and appliances.

"Hey, Cecil! Come look!"

Curious even as he protested, Cecil followed her into the kitchen. From there, they made their way into the dining room, living room, and eventually up the stairs. Aside from a few large pieces of furniture covered over with white sheeting, the house was emptied out. "Probably they moved their stuff into storage while they went away," Cecil surmised.

They glanced into the bedrooms, finding nothing of interest, and turned to leave. But Shelley noticed a handle on the ceiling indicating a pull-down trap door.

"We can't leave without exploring the attic," she insisted, eyes wide with guilty excitement. "We've come this far, and nobody's here."

He sighed and reached up for the handle. It responded to a slight tug, and the trap door transformed itself into a ladder, the upper rungs illuminated by sunlight

"Wow, it looks just like Jacob's ladder in the Bible stories!" Shelley exclaimed. Before Cecil could protest, she clambered up into the attic.

He followed reluctantly. A shaft of sunlight blazed through a small window, spotlighting the dust flurries stirred up by their entry. They stood hushed, suddenly humbled by their intrusion into the private stillness. They saw the usual attic curios, a wire dress form, an old window fan, a red vinyl toy chest, a wardrobe and bureau, and some boxes of books.

Cecil picked up one of the dusty volumes, rubbed his shirt over the cover, and read out loud, "The Song of Solomon: English German French." He flipped through the book. "It's really pretty, Shel, lots of colored pictures with tissue paper over them." He looked inside the front cover and whistled, "Wow, this book is from 1930!"

"Can you read it?"

Cecil scanned a few pages. "It's in three languages; let me find some English words. Here's some: 'Let him kiss me with the kisses of his mouth – for your love is more delightful than wine.'"

He paused, flustered. Shelley swung her foot and studied her shoe, trying to look nonchalant. "Read some more."

Cecil thumbed through, seeking a less intense passage, "'Arise, my darling, my beautiful one, and come with me.'" He looked up from the page. "Maybe we shouldn't be reading this."

She moved closer and examined the page, emboldened by his shyness.

"There's nothing wrong with reading about love, Cecil." She brushed her arm against his so that the tiny hairs stood on end. They stood near, listening to each other's breath, feeling each other's warmth, smelling the sweat and grit of the day's play, and appreciating the unfamiliar but pleasant stirrings.

His courage returned. He reached for her hand and found it surprisingly warm and soft. He leaned in closer and closer, until his face was nearly touching hers. Then he kissed her. Her eyes opened wide with surprise, but instinctively, she stood on her tiptoes and kissed him back. Suddenly bashful, she backed away.

Cecil laughed softly. "Gee, Shelley, I didn't mean to do that; it just happened."

"No, don't apologize! I liked it. Didn't you like it?"

He grinned. "Well, yeah, I liked it a lot."

They stared at the floor for a few seconds before he reached up with both hands and cradled her face, bending down to kiss her again.

Footsteps. Downstairs.

They jumped apart. Shelley's heart leapt into her throat

as Cecil looked at her with alarm. He pulled her behind the bureau. Holding a finger to his lips in a "shush" gesture, he wrapped his arm around her and they hunkered down, invisible to the intruder who had come up the stairs and paused at the open attic door.

"Could've sworn I closed this last time," said a soft voice.

They heard the sound of books being rustled in the boxes.

"Stupid Librarian," the voice muttered, "It's not my fault she can't keep her records straight. These folks won't mind if I borrow a few books while they're gone."

Cecil and Shelley remained still and quiet, hardly daring to breathe. At last the intruder's footsteps retreated back down the stairs. The trap door closed. They heard footsteps in the kitchen, the basement door opening and closing, muffled steps from further down in the basement.

Silence.

After waiting a few minutes to make sure they were alone, Cecil leapt up. "We have to get out of here!"

Shelley was already pushing on the trap door, lowering the stairs. They hurried through the house, into the basement and out the window, only pausing after they had run across the alley and down the street to her back yard. They leaned over, panting.

"That wasn't the owners!"

Cecil nodded. "I know, but we still don't want to get

caught in there!"

They avoided the empty house on the corner for the next few days, but neither could forget those sweet kisses. There just didn't seem to be anyplace where they could explore kissing in more earnest.

Finally, Cecil worked up the nerve.

"There are three rooms in the basement. We could bring in a blanket and have some privacy in the room away from the window. That way, if anyone came in, we'd hear them and they'd never see us, because they'd just head up the stairs."

Shelley couldn't see anything wrong with this plan. She was craving more of Cecil's attention, too. They met at the basement window that afternoon, Shelley carrying an old blanket rolled up under her arm.

Cozy and comfortable, they lay side by side, neither one knowing quite what to do next. It always looked simple enough on television.

Cecil figured it was probably his job to take the lead. He turned onto his side and reached for her. Shelley turned as well, and they kissed. One kiss led to another, and another, and then to caresses.

There was some fumbling of buttons and hands and limbs…some giggles and reassurances and gasps…and there on the soft blanket, in the dusky coolness of the deserted basement, Cecil and Shelley discovered clumsy, tender love.

A string bean Romeo and his prepubescent Juliet, hidden in the taboo darkness, reading to each other from the mysterious Song of Songs they had borrowed from the attic.

\#

"Wow, Grace, what's come over you? I don't recall you being so, well, enthusiastic before."

We lay entwined like naked pretzels on top of the my great-grandmother's quilt.

"I don't know, Hiram, I just think a little variety is the spice of life, you know? We don't always have to do the same things in the same way. There are lots of options."

"How do you know about any of that?"

"Oh, I've been doing some reading down at the Library. You'd be surprised what you can learn from some of those books!"

"I never would've thought you'd motivate me to go for seconds, and then thirds, all in the space of an hour."

I laugh with delight. "I'm thinking we can step into the shower together, and see what happens there. What do you say?"

He jumps up, grabs my hand, and we head into the bathroom.

\#

There was a lot of convincing going on around Water Street that summer. Cecil and Shelley convinced the younger children to stay away from the empty house by concocting a graphically gruesome ghost story. Vera convinced herself that it was OK to continue "borrowing" books from the boxes in the empty house's attic, never suspecting there were young lovers busy in the basement. And Mona convinced the lonely, middle-aged owner of the local diner that she was sixteen, which was not really necessary; he would have hired her, regardless.

Mr. D's was a two-counter eatery known for charbroiled hamburgers and thick soft serve ice cream. Mona, oddly demure in her beige uniform and white Keds, listened carefully as Betty, the old cook, gave her instructions. She was a quick study, and was soon working her own section of the counter, feeling confident.

But she hadn't quite understood the instructions about the soft serve ice cream machine. A monstrous silver hulk presiding over the two counters, it periodically ran out of milk. Mona's job included dragging the five-gallon milk bucket from the cooler, setting it on the counter, stepping onto a chair, hoisting the bucket over her head and pouring the contents into the top of the ice cream maker.

Betty helped her the first time.

Easy enough, Mona thought. The next time, Betty was busy, and Mona was impatient. She took a deep breath and lifted the bucket overhead, nearly falling off her chair as the milk sloshed from side to side. She steadied it, tilted it toward the top of the machine, and upended it completely.

But she had forgotten to first remove the lid on top of the ice cream maker. Cold milk cascaded over the ice cream machine and onto the row of customers sitting at the counter. They jumped up, sputtering and dripping. Mona, horrified at first, found the whole scene so funny that could barely choke back her laughter.

Mr. D. and Betty came running out of the kitchen, realized what had happened, and shouted, "Free burgers for everybody! Lunch on the house today!" while they handed out paper towels. Some of the more soaked customers left, but most remained and took advantage of the free meal.

One took special notice, wondering about the sparkling, young Venus in a waitress uniform.

Vernon worked as an appliance repairman, and made it a point to keep his blue uniform clean and pressed every day, so as to put his customers quickly at ease. He was a suave fellow in his early twenties, not bad looking.

He began frequenting Mona's section of the counter at Mr. D.'s. She wasted no time making up for her milky disaster, and earned a nickname as the "Banana Split Queen." Vernon became one of her regulars.

Over time, Mona took a shine to this man who always played her favorite song on the jukebox. He started inviting her to dinner. But she held out for his gift, which came in a sleek, gold box from the downtown jeweler. She opened it while protesting, "You shouldn't have!" and gasped with pleasure at the sparkly necklace and brooch set with her red birthstone.

"Now do you think your folks might let you have dinner

with me?" he coaxed. She pouted with feigned reluctance, but he persisted.

"We'll just be at the Elkhorn over by the Lake, Mona. It's not like I'm hauling you off to Shanghai or anything."

Mona had never been to the Elkhorn, Lamont's fanciest restaurant. She thought, *Now you're talkin'*.

"OK, I'll ask them."

Vernon and Mona fired off their romance with dinner at the Elkhorn, followed by a movie. The next weekend, they went out for an evening of miniature golf, then bowling. They sat in Vernon's parked car and necked while tippling from a bottle of vodka in a paper bag. Mona was impressed, but she still was determined to hold out for more.

Heck, maybe she should consider marrying this guy?

Cecil, on the other hand, was not impressed. "He's as slimy as a garden slug," he complained to Mona. "I don't like him."

She threw him a sisterly scowl. "Don't be silly, baby bro, I can handle myself."

"I'm helping Mr. Miller over at the bowling alley for spare change, and I get off the same time you leave Mr. D.'s. How about you let me walk home with you, Mona? I'd feel better."

She sighed and rolled her eyes. "Too sweet and so silly! OK, if it makes you feel better, you can walk me home and defend my honor, Cecil, but please don't cramp my style, OK?"

Cecil became Mona's companion as she walked the dark streets from Mr. D.'s to home.

Except for the night he and Shelley were so engrossed in their reading and etcetera that they lost track of the time.

Mona waited for him, but after twenty minutes had passed, she told Vernon, "My feet are killing me, and I need to get home."

"I'll walk you, dollface," Vernon offered.

She smiled at him and retrieved her purse. They chatted and held hands up to the dark intersection where a dirt path crossed the softball field over to the alley and home. Vernon tugged at her hand and stopped.

"What's wrong?" she asked.

He pulled her to him and started kissing her hard. She protested and pushed, but he held her fast.

"Vernon, stop! I want to get home."

"I can't stand your teasing anymore, Mona. You know you want it, too!"

Her temper flared. What gave him the right to force her into something? "Stop right now! I mean it, I'll scream!"

But he slapped her, a little harder than he intended, and fell on top of her. She found herself dazed, dizzy, and overpowered.

"Just try to relax, Mona, you'll enjoy it, I promise." He sat astride her hips and began pulling at her buttons.

In the basement of the empty house, Shelley sat up suddenly. "What was that?"

Cecil nuzzled her neck. "What was what?"

She pushed him away. "Wait! I heard something, like a horse's whinny."

Cecil laughed. "We don't have any horses around here. You're hearing things."

"Something's wrong, Cecil, I can feel it."

Shelley straightened her clothes, stood up, climbed onto the chair and scanned out the window into the yard. Cecil followed her, irritated at the interruption. Clouds shifted over the moon, playing tricks with the light.

Neither of them quite believed what they saw next: the shadowy shape of a man in dark clothing, galloping past them on a pale horse.

Cecil hissed a sharp intake of breath. "Holy Shinola! Did you see that?"

Shelley nodded, eyes wide and mouth agape, then sprung into action. "C'mon! We have to follow him! Bring that block of wood!"

They followed the impossible sound of muffled hoof beats to the softball field by the alley, where they saw two figures struggling. They rushed over. When Cecil realized he was watching Vernon assaulting Mona, he raised the wooden 2x4 and smacked him on the side of the head, knocking him off.

Sobbing with fear and anger, Mona pulled her skirt down as she got to her feet and kicked Vernon in the side. "You jerk! Don't you ever come near me again!"

Then she ran home, leaving Cecil and Shelley astonished and Vernon out cold.

The next day, Mona approached Shelley as she sat on
her porch swing. "I brought you somethin', honey. That was
brave what you and Cecil did last night, and I won't forget
it."

She handed Shelley a package wrapped in a small white
bag. Shelley opened it and was delighted to find a bright red
lipstick and matching nail polish. She beamed, "Cherries in
the Snow! Thanks so much!"

Mona smiled back. "You're not such a bad match for my
brother. The secret of your lovey-dovey rendezvous house is
safe with me. Good thing you guys decided to walk through
the softball field last night."

Shelley's smile froze. "Welllll, um, it's a strange thing
about that. We were sort of guided to you." She paused,
uncertain how much to say.

Mona's gaze sharpened. "Guided? Who guided you?"

"We, or rather I, heard a noise, like a horse would make.
And when we looked out, we both saw what looked like a
guy on a horse. I know it sounds crazy, Mona, but that's the
truth. We followed the sound of hoof beats, and they led us
to you in the field. I don't know anybody around here who
rides a horse, do you?"

Mona squinted her eyes and chewed her lower lip in
concentration. "A horse? In this neighborhood? Absolutely
no way that could happen without my knowing it."

Mona was baffled, but she knew Shelley wasn't one to make up stories. "Let's go ask Cecil what he saw."

Cecil wouldn't say much, but he affirmed that, "If it weren't for that shadow or whatever it was, I hate to think what would've happened. You may be tough, Mona, but Vernon's a lot stronger than you."

"You're right about that. I'm going to start learning self-defense. Maybe all girls should learn karate or kung-fu."

They all fell silent, lost in conjecture.

"Maybe it was a ghost!" Shelley shuddered.

"Must've been a friendly ghost, then," Mona said, "out rescuing people."

"I know. Maybe he was a miracle."

Cecil frowned.

"Well, they said in church that miracles can happen to anyone if you pray hard enough," Shelley insisted.

"Were you praying, Mona?" Cecil asked.

She shook her head, laughing. "When's the last time you saw me in church? Besides, I was pretty much knocked out. I hardly remember anything until you got there. So, baby bro, that makes about as much sense as little green men. But I suppose it can't hurt to imagine that we have a guardian ghost in the neighborhood."

She snapped her fingers and asked, "So who you wanna call?" then started humming her favorite tune as she half danced back to the house.

Inez emptied her glass, then stood up and stretched. "So that's the story, at least all I know of it. I can't explain what happened, but I'm grateful. It's nice to think that somebody out there is looking after us. Are you all staying for supper?"

As they drove away, Iris turned to her mom. "Why so deep in thought? You're not feeling guilty that we didn't eat there, are you?"

Lily shook her head. "No, it's not that. I just have the strangest feeling about Inez's story. Last year when Aurora came to visit mom, she told me about her notion that Abel has turned up as some kind of cowboy hero. She dreamed about him, and then one of her students described him, too. It's just weird, that's all, when you put it together with the story about Cecil and Mona."

❧✦❧

From atop his palomino stallion, a large man dressed in black laughs out loud and tips his hat.

"Weird, huh? Hell's bells, I've been called worse. You all didn't think I'd leave my folks to the wolves, did you? With Mona growing up to be such a looker, somebody has to watch out for her. She's got spunk, but no common sense. Not yet, anyway. And I never figured her dad to amount to much, sorry to say."

Abel wheels his horse around and trots into the mists, pointing his thoughts to a distant horizon.

Grace has company these days, with Hiram keeping her

occupied, and besides, she hasn't quite figured out The Crossover yet. I don't want to spook her. Think I'll head over to Calaveras and see if Mr. Clemens is up for a good gab, then maybe pan for gold near Truckee. Besides, Lake Tahoe is a real sparkler this time of year.

Chapter 10

Climbing El Capitan

1987

"Let's go over to the amusement park, Eureka, it will look all glittery with the snow, and we can make a real snow cone with some maple syrup. Besides we haven't ridden the carousel for I don't know how long."

The amusement park and the well are the two things that I didn't place in Possibilities, so naturally they fascinate me the most. The park is an exact replica of Abel's Place. I just came upon it one day. Spooked me so bad that I avoided it for a long time. Then when I ventured back to it, I just felt so dang homesick and nostalgic, I couldn't stand to be there.

All those rides sitting idle and memories of times past. Nothing is more sorrowful than an empty, quiet carousel, especially if you are acquainted with the ghostly images that seem to be lingering nearby.

But once I added families and all, it could be a pretty cheery pace to fritter away a day, so Eureka and I had returned there a few times.

Now I laugh as he runs to hide under the living room sofa.

"You're right. Our behinds would get frozen sitting on that yellow horse in this weather. How about this? We'll go ice skating. The creek is frozen over, I'll improvise a doggy sweater for you, and you can hide out in my bag. It'll be fun. We need something to get us going now that Hiram took off on his adventure to the big, wide world."

Oh, you're probably wondering what happened with Hiram. Well, we had a fantastic time. But after the novelty wore off, I realized we were falling into old patterns and ways. Kind of like trying to rediscover chapters of a book you've already finished reading. A bunch of times.

Besides, we had a half-century of marriage and life together, raised our kids, and said our goodbyes, all in the real world. Having more time began to feel like I was cheating life somehow, especially since he was made of dough and song and didn't know it.

I knew we had come to the end of it when I found myself tempted to call him "doughboy" as a little private pun. I mean, he never even fought in World War I because of his flat feet.

Bottom line? I was secretly relieved that the new Hiram had some unfulfilled aspirations. OK, you're right, I helped to plant those ideas. "Gee, Hiram, wouldn't you like to visit the Sphinx in Egypt? Or the fjords in Norway? Or what about that glow worm cave in New Zealand, can you imagine?"

I helped him prepare and pack, and we parted amiably

enough. But I am once again confronted with my solitude, and no end in sight.

So I'm delighted when, enroute to the creek, I over-hear familiar voices from the well. But they sound heated, urgent.

"They have to do what?" It's Luke.

Lily's voice is tight. "They have to amputate her left leg below the knee."

That gets my attention.

"Amputate? Why in God's name would they have to amputate the leg of a woman who has been lying in bed for over two years?"

A long silence, then finally Lily's voice again, choking with fury. "That new doctor removed a bunion, and it got infected, and her leg has gangrene, Luke!"

"Jesus H. Christ!"

"Stop swearing at me!"

"I'm not swearing at you, I just frickin' can't believe my ears. Who gave that doctor permission to even touch her?"

"We did, Luke, when we had her admitted there. He just took over for her other doctor. He says this was routine medical care. I've been visiting two, three times a week, and I had no absolutely no idea. All this time, I've been reading to her, and polishing her nails, and washing her hair, and keeping her tube site clean, and how could I not have noticed her leg was rotting? How could they not have no-ticed? I thought they were bathing her! Why didn't they tell me? It defies belief! Makes me sick! Sick! I demanded that she have a different doctor, but the new guy says that if he doesn't amputate her leg, she'll die of the gangrene."

A heavy sigh. "Lily, stop. Don't blame yourself. I know you've been running yourself ragged trying to be there for her and still keep up with your own life. I should have gone to see her more often, it's just that so much time passed with no change, and I've had so much work to do. But I have to believe that she's not aware of any of it. It's the only way I can stand to think of it at all! I think her mind is gone, and her body just can't give up the habit of breathing. I honestly don't believe she has suffered. I don't. I can't."

"That's fine for you, but, God! I'm afraid to let things go on like this. What else can they do to her when we're not looking? Maybe we should insist on a video camera or post an armed guard at her bedside twenty-four hours a day."

A third voice enters into the conversation. "Eureka, that sounds like Michael," I mumble, shaken and trembling. It seems like years since I've heard my younger son's mellow baritone. He sounds cool and collected, as usual.

"OK, here's the deal, everybody. I couldn't find another place within fifty miles that has an available bed. The only option close to here is a hospice, which means we would have to agree to disconnect Mom's life support in order for her to be eligible. Otherwise, it does sound like she'll need that surgery. If she stays here, they will assign a new doctor who seems really competent, Dr. Beaumont. I checked around. He's been in practice for about 20 years and he hasn't had any malpractice complaints."

"We need to seriously think about whether we want to put her body through an amputation, after everything else she's endured," Luke says. "Are we doing the kindest thing for her?"

Michael seizes on that line of thought. "That's the real question. She has no quality of life whatsoever. If I were her, I would want to stop this insanity and let me die with some peace…"

I listen, horrified. "Eureka, I think they're talking about taking away my feeding tube."

"… you can't possibly think that there's still a chance she'll wake up. The doctor has been really clear about that."

"Shut up, Michael," Lily snaps. "You're not in charge here. You haven't been around to visit Mother for months. What right do you have to come barging in and taking over?"

"Lily, arguing amongst ourselves doesn't change Mom's reality."

"I know, I know, it just seems so damn cruel, Luke. She's our mother!"

I sink to my knees in the wet snow, and Eureka jumps out of my bag. "They are! They're talking about taking away the tube that's keeping me alive."

The voices from the well continue arguing, debating, each trying to persuade the others of their point of view.

I pet Eureka and watch our breath turn to white vapor clouds that vanish in the grey air.

"How dare they! I gave them life, held their heads when they were sick, held their hands when they started kindergarten, held them all in my heart from the day they were born. All their lives I helped them, and here they are, ready to end me!

"But I don't really know how long it's been. What was that Luke said about 'two years?' More than two years? Have I really been unconscious for that long?" Time is so confusing here. Things just aren't, and then they are, as if they'd always been. Moments seem to last just as long as I want them to.

"They don't know what to do, and I can't help them. At the one time when we really need each other's help, they can't hear me, and I can't reach them.

"I know they love me, and they want to do the best thing. I hate that they have to see me on that bed, day in, day out. I hate that they live with the grief of it, dragging on their spirits like a ball and chain.

"But what will happen to you, and all of Possibilities, if I die? Will you all die, too? I can't stand to think of that! I feel responsible for all the people here. If my body dies, what's next? At least I have a wonderful life here, and some connection to them, if only through this infernal well."

Luke is speaking again, quietly now. "Lily, I'm sorry. But please stop acting like you're the only one who loves her. We all love her. We all miss her. But that isn't really her, lying in that hospital bed. How can it be her? Surely she has gone somewhere else, surely her spirit, her soul, whatever you want to call it, has escaped and is waiting to be totally free. Just because we want to keep her doesn't mean it's the right thing to do." His voice breaks. "We can't just let them keep taking pieces of her."

I hear Lily's continued sobbing through his words. A blackness closes in at the edges of my mind. I reel with the prospect of losing them, losing Possibilities, of being forever dead.

"Maybe they're right. After all, I haven't been able to open my eyes and look at them, much less talk with them, for a really long time. How awful for them, my children, being faced with this decision. And how awful for me, not being able to talk with them. Maybe it is time to shut me down."

Eureka whines and licks my hand, where my own tears are falling.

Another voice joins the children, measured and kind. "Folks, there is one more procedure I wanted to mention to you. It's a way of maybe stimulating your mother's brain with low voltage electrical current. It's highly experimental, and I don't want to raise false hopes. But if you feel as though you are prepared for things to go either way, perhaps ..."

"Yes!" Lily cries. "Whatever it is, we'll try it, so long as you can assure us it won't cause her any pain."

"No pain. It's no stronger than the tingle you feel with one of those electric neck massagers. If you are all in agreement, then I'll make the arrangements after she has the amputation."

I push myself up and stumble back to the house, where I brew a pot of coffee and cradle Eureka in the rocking chair.

"What's all this about amputating a leg?" I hold out my shapely calves. "Both legs looking good, if you ask me. And I feel fine. What are they talking about? And I wonder what the doctor has in mind. Seems like maybe there might be a chance to wake me up. Or not. Guess I'll find out soon enough. But how will I stand the waiting?"

✦

"Okay, Lily, let's just say all the hard things out loud. Mom's been unresponsive, in bed, for more than two years now. We did an MRI early on, which showed that her actual thinking brain, her cortex, was shut down already, and just her 'mechanical' brain was still working. Then we had that fancy thing, the PET scan, and it showed the same thing.

"Medically speaking, and for all intents and purposes, Mom's ability to think, to reason, to understand, to be herself, it's all long gone. So this is the last thing we try, do you agree?"

Luke took his sister's shoulders and turned her to face him straight on, so that he could detect any hint of resistance.

She stiffened and met his gaze. "Yes, I agree. I hear what you've been saying, I know how you feel, and to tell you the truth, I'm beginning to feel it, too. It's just been so hard to give up hope."

Relieved, Luke turned to his younger brother. "What about you, Michael?"

He nodded thoughtfully. "I think it's the best decision."

"Then we're in agreement on this. Okay, Doctor Beaumont, we're ready. Let's go ahead."

The doctor turned to his nurse and signaled for the equipment to be engaged. A soft hum calmed the air, and lights began blinking.

"How long until we know if there's a response?" Lily asked.

"We will be continually monitoring her for the next twenty-four hours," the doctor replied. "If there's anything, a brain wave, a twitch, a flicker, we'll know. These are just soft, gentle electrical urgings, if you will, to try and stimulate some brain wave activity. There's no pain, and no harm to her."

After the men left Grace's room, Lily sat in the rocking chair and prayed yet again for her mother to open her eyes. With a heavy sigh, she pulled an envelope out of her purse, just as she had done so many times over the past three years. The same number of times she had pretended that Grace could hear her. She began talking into the air.

"Mom, I have a letter from Connie Owens, do you

remember that little Sunday School student you had years ago? The one who thought that woman dressed up as the Virgin Mary was the real deal?" she laughed. "She was so cute."

Lily tsk'ed and shook her head. "Course, you remember she got hit by that drunk driver when she was in high school, right? What a shame. Broke her back pretty bad, I heard.

"Anyway, she's a physical therapist now. She just graduated and got a new job at the Veterans' Hospital in Minneapolis. Pretty neat, huh? I think you were a surrogate mother to her in some ways, you know, after her mom died when she was still little. I remember she was always picking your flowers and bringing them to the door as a present." Lily laughed again. "You looked pretty annoyed when she plucked your 'naked lady' lilies right off their stems!"

⚜

Despite the frigid weather and not wanting to hear any more bad news, I can't resist returning to the well. It's a comfort to hear Lily's voice, reading like always. I do recall little Connie, and how much fun it was, teaching Sunday School.

I snap an icicle off the well's roof and lean in to hear.

"Eureka, Lily's talking about that sweet little Connie, the one who used to keep bringing me my own flowers. She had some hard knocks, what with losing her mom early on, and then getting mowed down by that drunken lout. Sounds like she's doing pretty well, now, though." I pause, afraid to hope.

"And they're trying that newfangled thing today. To wake me up."

Eureka stretches, shivers and barks at me. "You're right, it's too cold to hang out here. Let's go put some beans in the pressure cooker."

I've discovered that old rituals are still soothing.

"The smell of brown sugar baked beans will cheer up the whole house. I'll call Doris and invite her over for dinner. Maybe it will take my mind off of things I can't do anything about."

⚜

"OK, Dad, thanks for letting me know. I do want to come for the services if she dies."

Connie hung up the phone, grimly telling herself, "when she dies." She knew it was unlikely that Grace would emerge from a coma that had persisted for this long.

She found herself thinking back to long afternoons under the soft click and flickering shadow of a huge ceiling fan in the Iowa Sunday School, her feet swinging free from the hard wooden chair while she sucked on peppermint candies that Miss Grace handed out.

Poor Miss Grace, confined in her body like that. Connie had come close to being confined in her body, herself. She shook her head and forced herself to concentrate.

"First day at a new job, I need to be alert." She sighed deeply, then straightened her shoulders and limped into the hospital's Physical Therapy office to check in.

"Here you go." The nurse handed her the patient roster. "Some new admits, and some long timers."

"They're all new to me," Connie said, smiling. "Wow, here's a guy who's been here for a long time. Sergeant Benjamin Reyes."

The nurse faced Connie with her hands on her hips and laughed. "Fifteen years. Longer than me, and that's saying something. His history is all there, if you have time to read it." Connie opened the file and started skimming the medical notes as she headed for the Rehab Unit. It wasn't all there but she could fill in the missing details.

It started in 1972. A stealthy little virus hitchhiked a ride from a pile of dog poop to Sergeant Benjamin Reyes's mouth, probably with the help of a fly that landed first on the excrement, then on the rim of his coffee cup in Saigon. Benjamin was happily anticipating his transfer to stateside, going home to his wife and two sons in Minneapolis. Chances are he took no notice of the fly, probably waved it off while talking and laughing with his buddies. He thought nothing of it as he went back to his barracks, retrieved his bags and headed for the airport, where he boarded a military transport to Hawaii, laid over for a few days of rest and recreation, then continued to Los Angeles before finally arriving home to the delight of his family.

The fly couldn't have been further from his thoughts a few weeks later, when Benjamin developed a fever, severe headache and neck stiffness, badly aching muscles, and tingling in his arms and legs. He likely figured it was a bad cold, maybe the flu.

He had no inkling that intruder cells were multiplying in the lymphoid tissue of his throat and stomach. Nor did he realize those cells entered his bloodstream, from where they made their way into the central nervous system, inflaming his spinal cord and brainstem and systematically attacking motor nerve cells.

When the polio virus was finished working him over, Benjamin was left with spinal paralysis, rendering him quadriplegic. He regained some limited head and face mobility with intensive physical therapy, but never reacquired movement of his limbs.

Once he comprehended the full impact of his condition, he was bitterly grateful to have retained the ability to breathe, swallow and speak, especially since the residually intact mouth movement made it possible for him to maneuver a specially outfitted wheelchair.

And now he was listed, along with three others, on Connie's rehabilitation duty roster at the Minneapolis Veterans Administration Medical Center.

She entered his room and beheld a small, balding figure lying in bed with a hulking wheelchair nearby. He looked up and smiled at her in a way that invited her to come closer.

"Heooeryeoo?" His speech was mangled; "dysarthric," Connie reflected on the medical term.

"I'm Connie, your new Physical Therapist. Just thought I would stop by and say hello before starting our work tomorrow."

He grinned broadly and nodded his head in acknowledgement. "Am 'en" he offered in an unintended parody of a prayer's ending, but she understood; she already knew his name was Benjamin.

"Nice to meet you, Ben," she said while scanning the gadgets and paraphernalia around his bed. She pointed to the radio. "What do you have here?"

"S-S-SeeBee!" he smiled with pride, and lifted his chin to indicate she could put on the headphones. "Eyeyit."

She put on the headphones and found herself listening to police radio calls.

"Yeookaearairpaneteoo!"

She was figuring out his speech patterns. "No kidding! Do I just turn the dial?"

He nodded. She adjusted the radio control and tuned in to the tower at Minneapolis/St. Paul airport, then listened to a brief exchange between an incoming pilot and an air traffic controller.

"That is so cool!"

He nodded emphatically, still smiling. She wondered if he was able to refrain from smiling, or if it was a permanent muscle contraction. Or maybe he'd had a stroke that left him brain damaged, in a permanently, ridiculously happy state of mind.

Connie looked around the room. There were photographs of a younger Ben with his wife, images of two young men in their high school graduation robes, and a boldly colored print of El Capitan at Yosemite. He saw her studying it and asked, "Climb?"

She smiled and shook her head. "Not me, Ben, I get vertigo in high places. I'm too wimpy to even do the cable climb up Half Dome." No sense in telling him about her bad back and limp, the result of being hit by a drunk driver while still in high school.

He smiled back, "I climb, someday."

It occurred to her that Ben was deliberately using telegraphic speech, for his sake and hers.

Makes him sound like Yoda, she thought. Especially with that moon face and bald head.

They fell silent for a moment, both considering their personal obstacles. Her eye landed on a Hollywood studio portrait hanging on the wall. The actor's face was pockmarked but handsome in a craggy way, topped off by a bristly mustache. Dressed all in black, he was leaning forward with a look that said, "Go on, I dare ya'."

Connie thought she recognized the face. "He reminds me of that guy that used to be on TV, one of the cowboy westerns. The one that wasn't dumb as dirt."

Ben smiled in appreciation. "My hero."

"Yeah, mine, too! I used to sneak down the stairs and peek through the banister to watch the show while my parents thought I was asleep. What was his name? I heard he got a ton of fan mail from the ladies. I guess he's dead now, huh?"

"Still here!" Ben insisted, inclining his chin to the photograph.

"And here," she gestured to her heart, feigning a love-sick expression. They laughed together.

Relieved they had moved away from the depressing topic of their shared inability to climb El Capitan, Connie closed her clipboard, made a note in Ben's medical chart, and looked up. "I should probably get going; I have other patients to meet. How about if I come back tomorrow morning at 9:00?"

He lifted his eyebrows to indicate agreement, and she left.

Connie worked with Ben twice a week for half-hour sessions, following the series of activities recommended by his previous therapist. Most of these involved limb stretching/manipulating, head, neck, eye and mouth mobility practice, and other movements designed to help keep his muscles from further rigidity or atrophy.

He would often greet her with a comment about the gorgeous weather, the need to get out of the stuffy hospital atmosphere, or the offer to treat her to an ice cream at the commissary, where his family ensured that his account was amply funded. The mouth-driven wheelchair afforded him relative independence as they made their way around the hospital grounds.

He's amazingly good company.

Ben was always happy to be outdoors, willing to go wherever he could maneuver his wheelchair, and keenly observant. In order to save his energy, and the patience of others, Ben had learned to think first and carefully choose the most loaded words and phrases.

Connie found herself following his example, so that they had brief, pithy conversations consisting largely of amiable silence.

I imagine that communication and life in general would be much improved if the whole world used language this way. I wonder if he's always looked like a happy Buddha, or if it's the result of years of paralysis and limited social involvement.

Ben had round, rosy cheeks, sparkling brown eyes framed by high arching eyebrows and a ready smile with dimples. His demeanor was almost childlike in its sincerity. Sometimes when she arrived at his door, she detected some sadness, but upon seeing her, his face lit up with a beaming smile that stretched from ear to ear. No one had ever made her feel so welcome.

Every so often, she found herself moseying into his room, unscheduled, just to enjoy that smile and comically grotesque articulation, "Coeee!"

Ben was intensely interested in other people's life stories. Over time, he elicited hers. "Your mom?"

"She died of influenza when I was only two." A familiar
pang of being cheated.

He was too empathetic to insult her with pat
condolences.

"And Dad?"

"Dad's alive and well. He's a veterinarian. Dad has a
kind heart, but I've always felt that he's more comfortable
with animals than with people. He means well, and he was
a great Dad and all, but we have a hard time talking about
the tough topics, if you get my drift."

Ben nodded thoughtfully. "Any other mom?"

She looked at him, surprised, then smiled. "Yes, you're
right. Corny as it sounds, my Sunday School teacher was
kind of a second mom. Her name was Miss Grace, and she
was very cool. She did her best to make me into a good
Catholic, but I was a challenge."

Ben waited, eyebrows raised.

"You know, she said the ladies had to wear head cover-
ings in church, but I noticed that the guys didn't have to,
so that seemed unfair. Then she told me that the holy water
was special because that man in a bathrobe touched it, and
I couldn't buy into that. Then she said that same guy would
talk to God for me, and I told her I could talk to God myself
just fine. Things like that."

"How old were you?"

"About 8, I guess. Maybe I was already a little mad at God for letting Mama die. Anyway, after they tricked me into thinking the Virgin Mary was coming to visit, and it turned out to be a lady wearing a scarf on her head, that was pretty much it for me. I told Grace I felt closer to God outdoors than in church."

Ben laughed. "Was she mad?"

"No, not at all. I remember we were sitting in her porch swing one night, all cozy under her big afghan, picking out the constellations. That's when I told her about feeling closer to God outdoors, you know, with the stars twinkling and the crickets chirping and all.

"And she said, 'You know, honey, Jesus said that in God's house there are many mansions.' I could see her hands gesturing in the dark. 'I figure that means there are lots of ways to be with God, and we all have to find the one that works for us. So if outdoors is where you talk to God, then that's OK. Just be sure you're also listening. You have to give God equal time, you know.'"

Ben nodded slowly. "Smart lady."

"She really was. She tried to make all the Bible stories apply to modern life, and listened when kids were having trouble and needed to talk. She was there for at least four years. And she let me hang out at her place a lot, like I was one of her own."

Connie smiled, thinking back to good times on the farm.

"Oh, and she was a fantastic baker. I loved spending

summer afternoons in her kitchen, helping her bake pies and cakes, and just talking. I used to go into her garden and pick her flowers, then bring them to her as a gift! She never once scolded me for picking them."

She thought about Grace's abusive and botched medical care and choked down her rage. Ben had enough troubles without hearing bad news.

"Your back, Connie?"

Surprised, she asked, "How did you know?"

He lowered his eyes and shrugged.

She blushed. Of course he would notice something like a crooked back and a limp.

"I was hit by a drunk driver when I was kid. The doctors did their best, but it just never healed properly."

"Hurts?"

"A little when the weather's changing, but usually it's OK."

"Driver?"

"Oh, they caught him, and he lost his license, but honestly it didn't make much difference. He kept driving anyway, and he never went to jail."

Ben shook his head with a rare frown.

Connie's thoughts whirled back to that rainy night, walking home from the gymnasium, humming "Cinnamint" while she danced through the steps of her cheerleader routine. Behind her, a car's engine revved loudly, speeding too fast on the slick pavement … a terrible screech as she turned

… a giant fist hit her in the chest and she was suddenly airborne…and then… darkness. Next thing she knew, there was a siren, flashing red lights, blood in her mouth, mud between her fingers, rain pelting her face, people in white jackets shouting her name, telling her not to move. As if she would, with all that pain.

Connie's gaze refocused on Ben, patiently watching her. She squirmed, wondering how much honesty either of them really wanted.

"He took a lot from me, Ben. Never mind the team sports, gymnastics, swimming, dancing. The doctors said I would never walk again. I spent years in physical therapy, and even now my back aches. If it weren't for all that medical help and a really good yoga teacher, I'd be seriously disabled. I've never truly forgiven him."

He looked pointedly at her, then slowly scanned his withered legs and useless arms.

The old anger flared. "I hate what happened to you, Ben. But I also hate what happened to me. Why should I forgive him? He walked away that night, and never looked back!"

"Darkens your mind. Pulls you down."

She shook her head with a wry smile. "Let's head back, OK? I need to leave pretty soon."

They returned to his room in uncomfortable silence. Connie's feelings were bruised, but her pride even more so.

How dare he?

But…what if he's right?

To her relief, Ben seemed fine with normal banter after that. One day they were enjoying the breeze on the hospital lawn when she told him that she had been asked to take over a friend's yoga class in the prison at Stillwater.

"Why you? You work, should rest!" It was one of the few times she saw him look worried.

"It will be a great experience; probably teach me some appreciation for my own blessings in life, and besides, it's a form of giving back, you know. I'll tell you all about it next week."

\#

Over baked beans and coconut cake, I promise Doris I'll join her the next day and help her with a quilt. After she leaves, I clean up the kitchen and fret.

Good grief, I can't just hang around that blasted well night and day! Oh, phooey. Just a quick listen.

I put on my wool coat, gloves and galoshes, and tromp out the back door, Eureka trailing reluctantly behind me. We trudge through the heavy snow along the path from the back door to the well. I lean over and shiver as the cold air frost-burns my nostrils.

Chapter 11

Incarceration

"Hey, that's Connie talking. She was my Sunday School student who wrote the letter Lily was reading earlier today."

I don't know what's wrong with me, I'm just yearning for some familiar closeness, and my nerves are frayed raw to bleeding. It couldn't hurt to just pop into Connie's thoughts for a second.

But you promised! Not anymore with live people. Especially when they're awake.

I'll just check in, fast, and get out. I'm so sorrowful I can't stand it.

So I focus, hum, feel the familiar vibration and shift, then find myself looking out at the world through her eyes.

⚜

A crisp, sunny Saturday in October. Connie spent an hour getting dressed, putting on three layers of clothing that completely hid any semblance of a female figure.

Looking in the mirror, she was satisfied to behold an amorphous blob with hands and feet. Then she secured her hair up on top of her head, covered it with a white gauze wrap, and added a neck pouch of lucky stones.

"A casual observer would think that I'm some kind of

Celtic witch headed out to do battle with the forces of evil," she muttered to herself.

Next she gathered up her yoga mat, a book of poems and readings, an audiocassette player, some calming music, and her nerve, before finally leaving her apartment in St. Paul for the prison in Stillwater.

Forty minutes later, she pulled into the prison entrance and parked the car. She gathered all her gear, took a deep breath and went inside.

In a large anteroom, she passed through a metal detector and was wanded by a guard, then went through an electronically operated door that led her to a smaller room with more guards. They conducted a manual search of her belongings while confirming that her visit was logged on the day's roster, before waving her forward to the third and final door.

The 2-inch thick, 12-gauge steel obelisk swung ponderously open from floor to ceiling, then clanged shut behind her. Connie suppressed an urge to turn around, pound her fists and yell for immediate release.

She was officially inside the Minnesota Correctional Facility at Stillwater, the state's largest Level Four institution for men, housing approximately 1,400 inmates. All in maximum security.

Connie had done her homework. She knew that the prisoners' offenses ranged from white collar crime such as forgery or fraud, to kidnapping and robbery, to criminal sexual assault and homicide.

Aside from the 180 prisoners serving life sentences (with or without the possibility of parole), other inmates' average length of sentence was approximately 12 years.

She surveyed the long, wide hall ahead of her, flooded with daylight, which opened onto three tiers of cellblocks. She followed closely behind an armed escort, wondering what in the world she was doing here.

Contemplating the unsavory prospect of walking past the cellblocks, she was relieved when the escort immediately turned left at a large carved oak door. He gestured for her to enter.

"Here's the Chaplain's office. They're waiting for you already. I'll be posted right here outside the door if you need anything," he said. Connie stifled the urge to ask him to wait inside the room rather than outside the door. At least he would be within earshot.

She opened the door and found herself in a surprisingly inviting room. Approximately fifteen feet square, with sparse furnishings pushed against the wall, carpeted and fully enclosed with no windows, it was, in fact, a hushed and peaceful space.

Seated cross-legged on the carpet were five men of assorted sizes and ethnicities, calmly waiting. They had left an open space in the middle of the carpet, presumably where they were accustomed to having a teacher seated.

Connie mentally revised her planned routine; these

guys looked like they were expecting a real workout, not just wimpy stretches.

She rolled out her mat, smoothed the wrinkles, placed the book nearby, set up the tape player and looked around for an electrical outlet, whereupon one student arose to help, then resumed his seat. After several minutes of this fussing and fidgeting, she finally worked up the courage to look each of them in the eye.

"Hi, I'm Constance, and I'm here in place of James today."

They all smiled, indicating they had known she was coming, and one by one, told her their names.

She led them through a yoga set consisting of some opening meditation with deep breathing, then some vigorous warm-ups, moving into more intense stretches and isometric postures, balances, a cool down, and closing meditation, pretty standard stock for a well-rounded yoga class.

Exactly one hour later, the guard knocked on the door and entered the room, signaling her students to return to the main prison complex. Hands in prayer position at chest level, they bowed to her with the traditional phrase, "namaste," and she returned the blessing, then watched them file out.

She looked around the room and let her body go slack. After all the fretful anticipation, the actual class ran so smoothly that it felt almost anticlimactic.

Connie sat for a few minutes on the carpet, then rolled up her mat, gathered the book and tape player, and accompanied the guard back to the gigantic security door. She waved to the guards, who nodded, then stepped back through the smaller door into the lobby, and emerged into the parking lot, where she paused to take a deep breath.

The day was picture postcard beautiful, billowy clouds in an azure sky set off by flaming red maple trees, and the air smelling of burning leaves.

Feeling inexplicably guilty, Connie drove to a Dairy Queen and ordered onion rings and a chocolate malt before heading back to Minneapolis.

The next week, Ben listened thoughtfully when she told him about the class. "Go back?" he asked.

"I don't know, maybe. I don't think there's anyone else to continue teaching the class, and they seem to be pretty serious students."

He nodded. "Careful."

"I know, but I think it's pretty safe, Ben. I don't even really go into the main part of the prison. It's not like I'm walking by all the cells or anything, like in the movies where the prisoners make whistles and catcalls at the lady attorney. These guys are more respectful than some of the students in my regular yoga classes!"

Connie became the regular teacher for Saturday morning yoga classes at Stillwater prison. Over time, she learned that all of her students were incarcerated for murder, and caught snatches of stories involving misplaced loyalty, desperate passion and bad choices.

Listening to their banter after class ended, Connie reflected that they were a baffling blend of courtesy and lack of conscience. She had never known a group of people who were so badly in need of an epiphany.

But, I'm not kidding myself. I don't think my yoga classes will be enough to give them one.

One morning at the hospital, Ben and Connie were wheeling back to his room when he stopped his chair and peered up into a tree. They both listened to a robin singing his personal opus.

"In yoga, they teach that certain sounds can heal us," she mused to Ben, who smiled.

"Birdsong," he asserted, "cleans your mind, heals your soul." Then he coughed.

She glanced at him. "That cough seems to be getting worse. I'm going to ask your doctor to check it out."

He pursed his lips in dismissal. "Nothing," he said, then coughed again. "Tired."

But he was more than tired. After fifteen years of restricted mobility, Ben's lungs and chest wall had lost elasticity, so that he wasn't taking full breaths. He fatigued more quickly, and complained of headaches and depressed mood.

He contracted a respiratory infection and fought it off with the help of antibiotics, but then relapsed, this time declining into pneumonia.

When she went to see him in his room, the nurse advised Connie that Ben had been transferred to Intensive Care. That night, she found herself praying for him to get well, all the while feeling selfish because maybe it would be better for him to be released from his body after all this time of being incapacitated.

≈❖≈

Just as I try to settle into Connie's thoughts, I'm jarred with the sudden awareness that I'm not the only visitor there. I can sense a large presence who thinks of himself as "Ben." A familiar sense of immobility jolts me, as I realize that Ben is locked into his body, just as I'm locked into mine. But he is fully conscious.

How does he stand it?

And there's something else about him; a gentleness. I can feel his ability to soothe others, despite his own infirmity. His essence feels like a warm compress on an achy muscle. Nonetheless, his voice in my thoughts is startling.

"Nice to meet you, Grace."

Feels like I've been caught trespassing, but even worse is the sudden fear that I've somehow become stuck in Ben's thoughts, or Connie's, or both.

"Don't worry; we won't get stuck. I've been doing this for a while now. You can relax and let me drive."

"Have we met?"

"Not exactly. I'm able to access your thoughts through

Connie, because she loves you. Love makes a good conduit. The best, actually. You just need to practice a little more detachment in order to maintain yourself and not get stuck."

"I've been thinking about Connie. After that horrible accident, I worried that her anger would fester into bitterness."

"Not completely, but there is some of that."

"Can you help her? I don't seem to be able to reach anyone from my current state, wherever it is. I can hear people through this well, but it only works in one direction, and whatever I drop into it vanishes."

"The well isn't for you to talk through, Grace. It's for nourishing your spirit, kind of like the gastronomy tube is nourishing your body. At some point, you'll have to choose which one is more important to you, and which one you're willing to sacrifice, your spirit or your body. Yelling or dropping things into the well isn't enough, won't ever be enough." Ben pauses. "But I can help her. Don't worry."

⚜

Connie visited Ben with a heavy heart. The ICU room was a bland mélange of cream, white and beige. There were two rolling bed trays littered with the paraphernalia of sponge baths, clean plastic bottles of saline solution, and a small cassette player emitting some New Age jazz music.

Looks like the family's been in to visit him.

Ben rested in a bed that mechanically adjusted itself

with a quiet hum every so often, a strangely mechanical lullaby. He was surrounded by intravenous stands hung with multiple plastic bags of pastel liquids, while flat monitor screens listed the running records of his heartbeat and oxygen saturation, punctuated by beeps.

Behind him was a floor to ceiling column into which all the power cords attached, like a stoic, imposing guardian feeding electrical juice to all the equipment for his medical care.

Under the tastefully cheerful print of his hospital gown, Ben's body seemed fleeting, gossamer, a diminutive mound attached to his round face.

Which was smiling at her, as always.

"Connie! Hope you come. Left El Capitan, cowboy pictures downstairs. Bring up here?"

She hurried down to his room, retrieved the pictures, and propped them up on the swiveling stand near his bed. He beamed. "You angel."

He lowered his voice and looked conspiratorial. "Listen. A secret. I saw ghosts."

She stared at him, worried that he was starting to hallucinate. "What do you mean, ghosts?"

"Not crazy. People floating around my bed."

Connie's heart skipped a beat. "I'm afraid of ghosts, Ben. Are they scaring you?"

He shook his head emphatically. "No, no! Seem nice. One said 'Connie.'" He looked triumphant, as if he had just pulled a rabbit out of a hat.

"Ben, are they giving you morphine? It can make you have really vivid dreams, almost like hallucinations. Why would a ghost come floating by and say my name?" He was scaring her a little with all this talk.

"Your teacher still alive?"

With a start she recalled the conversation about Miss Grace. She still hadn't told him the whole story, about the abuse in the nursing homes, or even that Grace was in a coma.

"Well, yes and no. She got really sick, and I guess she's comatose or something. You're not suggesting that she came to you as a ghost, are you? You know how crazy that sounds, right?" she teased softly.

He smiled and yawned. "Not ghost. Maybe spirit. Sweet spirit. Loves you. Not scary. Probably just dreams," he said, closing his eyes. Then he continued, "Connie, you take both pictures, yours." He began to doze.

Ben's doctor told Connie point blank that Ben was dying and wouldn't likely survive the week. Every night she resolved to talk with him frankly about death, because she had heard people say how important that was. She wanted him to know how much he meant to her, how his spirit had uplifted hers countless times during their work together, and how much she would miss talking with him.

But somehow the words never came. They spoke of the day's weather, and the traffic jam caused by an overturned molasses truck, and the new nurse's provocative hemlines. Some might say they both chickened out.

Or perhaps they both understood that the feelings about death can never be neatly wrapped up in words. *Maybe sometimes,* Connie thought, *death is like riding a weary train uphill, and the best you can do for someone is ride along with them until it gratefully slows to a stop at the top of the hill and starts the next leg of its journey, but you can't go any further.*

⤝❖⤞

I stomp the snow off my boots in the back entryway and huff into the kitchen, feeling satisfied about helping Doris finish her quilt. I had left Eureka behind, as he isn't fond of the Hansens' German shepherd.

I never should have baked up that big kalumper, but she was missing him.

I also know how much he enjoys snooping the yard when I'm not around to scold him. Besides, he wouldn't go far in this cold. I stand on the back porch and catch snowflakes on my tongue, then look around.

"Eureka! Time to get home!"

I hear his whine, and follow the sound out to the well, where I stop dead in my tracks. Even in the dark I can see him struggling, tangled in the frayed rope pulleys, and dangling precariously over the dark space below. My heart pounds as I run over to free him. But I can't quite reach!

"What on earth happened? Oh, sweetie, were you

chasing the birds again? Thank God your leg went into the loop."

I scold and reassure him, trying not to sound scared. He whimpers, frightened and begging for rescue.

"Hold still, I'll get the stepstool and free you up."

He begins barking frantically. I lumber as fast as I can in the deep snow, berating myself for staying so long at Doris's.

"Hold still," I holler to him.

But he's too panicky, and continues squirming. As I pick up the stepstool and plough my way back, I hear a desperate yelp echoing from the walls of the well, and icy dread floods my heart.

The water shimmers and shines like always, the surface undisturbed.

Absolute stillness.

Peering down into the damnably smooth water, I begin wailing desperately, willing with all my being for him to surface. He knows how to dog paddle. Where is he? I could throw him the rope, even though it's frayed. He's small, tiny even. He could seize it with his mouth. I could pull him up!

But in my gut I know.

Nothing comes out of that well. Nothing. Eureka has vanished, just like my voice, the penny, the rocks, the yarn, the notes, my hope. All gone.

My fists ball up in fury.

"NOOOO!" I hammer on the well's stone. "Give him back! You can't have him! GIVE HIM BACK! No, no, no, no . . ."

I crumple to the ground with sobs. He was my first creation, my first friend here.

"You don't need him, you horrible, stinking well! Nourish my spirit? All you do is swallow things up! You even swallow my voice so no one can hear me. You're a thief! You just rob and steal!"

Full of rage, I start hurling loose dirt and rocks at the well.

"You didn't need to shut down my body! And you didn't need to let a rapist loose in a nursing home! And you didn't need to cut off my leg! Who are you? What is wrong with you? You horrible, evil rot! I hate you! How dare you even be here in my yard? Get out! Get out of my yard, get out of my LIFE, you stinking, demonic THING! GET OUT!"

Absolute stillness.

At last, exhausted and sick with grief, I fall back onto the snow.

"A million miles away. I'm a million miles away from everything and everyone I love."

I wonder how the world could change so much with so little fanfare, in the blink of an eye.

❧✦❧

Ben was smiling at Connie, when suddenly his gaze

went blank. The heart monitor's steady beep lapsed into an unrelenting whine, and the light in the room dimmed almost imperceptibly. By the time the crash cart rushed in, he was gone.

She had a brief thought about the world changing so much with so little fanfare, in the blink of an eye.

At that moment, she heard the distant whinny of a horse, and a man's voice, as if soothing the animal.

Oh, brother, she chided herself, but an involuntary tremor passed through her as she glanced at the photograph of Ben's cowboy. *Say Hello to him for me, Ben, tell him you're both my heroes.*

She retrieved his two favorite pictures, trudged out to the hospital parking lot, and left for home. Her stomach growled at her for skipping lunch. The streetlights blurred through her tears.

Ben's family decided to hold his Memorial Service in the hospital chapel, because so many of the staff members wanted to come and couldn't get the day off.

Connie entered the chapel that afternoon to find it overflowing with at least fifty people. *How did he know so many people?* she wondered. *He couldn't go any further than the Hospital commissary.*

The next day, with her Stillwater yoga students, after the opening meditation, Connie was embarrassed to find herself bursting into tears. The guys were stunned into awkward silence.

Finally, one of them handed her a box of Kleenex from the minister's desk.

"Hey, Teach, slow down," he said gruffly. "Crying towels are not provided by the management here, you know."

The others exhaled and waited until she calmed down to sniffles.

"What's up?" the youngest one asked.

She took a deep breath.

"There was this guy I've been working with at the Veteran's Hospital in Minneapolis, his name was Sergeant Reyes ... "

"Hey!" interjected a Latino student. "'Reyes' means 'King' in Spanish!"

"That's perfect," she smiled.

When she finished telling the story about Ben, and how he had made such a positive difference for so many people who knew him, even while confined to a bed in a hospital for fifteen years, they all stared at the floor, not knowing what to say.

Finally, the translator spoke up. "Wow, that dude really was like a King, like supernatural or something."

Connie laughed. "Maybe. He certainly had a unique mind and spirit."

"I can't imagine living like that!" another chimed in. "No way to move your arms or legs, that would be worse than being in jail!"

She shrugged. "Maybe there are all kinds of prisons. You

can be locked up behind bars, or locked up in a sick or injured body. Ben once told me that you can even be locked up in yourself because you're too scared, or too greedy, or judgmental or bitter."

She reflected on the prickly conversation she shared with Ben about not forgiving the drunk driver who left her broken and bleeding on the roadside so many years ago. She continued talking aloud, more to herself than to them.

"Ben would say that anger and revenge are just different kinds of prisons. Maybe when you dwell on how people did you wrong, or how life dealt you a lousy hand, or you think about getting even, it drains your energy for the good things."

"Revenge is sweet," one of them asserted, and a few others nodded in assent.

She shook her head and regrouped her thoughts. "People get locked up all kinds of ways, that's all I'm saying. There are all kinds of prisons."

"But that guy, he reached out of his prison," another student reminded them, "even though he couldn't move, he mattered to people. He mattered to you, Constance, and you weren't even his family. He was an inspiration, man, he inspired everyone he knew."

They fell silent again, and she realized that now Ben had inspired them, these men who would never meet him. Despite his imprisonment in life, Ben had reached out from beyond death and given them their epiphany.

Chapter 11

Dance the Beguine

1987

I come to awareness lying in the snow next to the well, after I don't know how many frozen sunsets. Oddly enough, I feel hungry and thirsty. My hands and feet have moved past cold to painful, and are now thankfully numb.

At least a foot of new snow has fallen, and I recall a vague memory about a local farmer who went to sleep in the snow and died of hypothermia.

Who cares? Sounds like a peaceful way to go. After all, I'm as good as dead in that other world, so why worry about freezing to death in this one? Maybe I'll just make myself comfortable.

Through the miasma of despair, I catch snatches of my children's discussion coming up from the accursed well.

"We agreed, Lily, this would be the last thing, the last hope, we agreed! Let her go, Lily!"

I try to rouse myself.

I need to let them know about Possibilities before they decide to let me die.

Shaking and weak, I lean over the side of the well, smelling its hollow dampness and searching the secretive water in vain for some kind of reflection. From somewhere below the water, the voices continue arguing.

"Who are you to play God?" Lily's voice.

"I can't stand it anymore! Hasn't she been through enough?" That was Luke.

Then Ben's voice interjects itself into my thoughts. "The well isn't for you to talk through, Grace. It's for nourishing your spirit. At some point, you'll have to choose which one you're willing to sacrifice, your spirit or your body. Yelling and dropping things in isn't enough, won't ever be enough."

Fear grips me as I realize what I've been avoiding all along.

I have to jump in.

It's just that the well is so bizarre, and ... I can't swim.

Then I hear another voice, the cowboy who helped me get loose from Abby's fractured thoughts. The one who winked at me.

"Get a rope, Grace. One that's strong enough to hold you."

A rope! I stumble to the barn and find the heavy rope coiled on the same nail Hiram hammered into the wall, who knows how many years ago. I secure one end to the top of the well, throw the other end into the moist darkness, and test my weight on it.

Maybe I should get an umbrella, I think, absurdly, and shake my head. *Get a hold of yourself, Gracie.*

I pull off my boots, check for the tattered prayer book reliably secured in my coat pocket, and climb up to balance on the edge of the well. My toes curl in protest to the icy rim of stone.

I feel renewed loathing at how the water's shimmering opacity seems to mock me.

Why doesn't this well have any reflection? It's just evil. I should at least be able to see the moon; it's full as a marshmallow.

My oldest son's voice echoes from below. "I'm sorry, Lily, it's the best thing for her and for us. You think I'm being a monster now, but you'll thank me after this is all over."

Then the cowboy's voice chimes in, again. "You can do it, Grace. You're The Baker. It's time."

More terrified than I've ever been, I grab the rope with one hand, plug my nose with the other, shut my eyes, and step forward into the well.

I am floating, disembodied, a will-o-the-wisp, a passion, a whim, a moment, an con. I am everything and nothing…but it's not enough.

So I open my eyes to the fuzzy white blur of a dandelion swaying in the breeze over my face. It is one of many in a warm, sweet smelling field of grass near the amusement park in Possibilities. Off in the distance, I hear carousel music, Laughing Sal, and a crowd cheering to the crack of a home run hit over on the baseball field. I'm wearing my gingham sundress, and pink sandals with the straw flowers on them. I sit up, stretch, and wonder where my winter clothes have gone. Dazed, I stand and slowly head off toward the carousel.

There I come upon a man dressed in black, currying a large palomino stallion.

"I don't believe it. I saw you! You helped Abby in Las Vegas!"

He turns to look at me. "Helped you, too, didn't I? You looked a little stranded there in her mental muck. I've lent a hand to some of your other people, too. Remember that skunk of a Professor who was slobbering over your granddaughter? The guy who got caught with his fly open, and arrested by a mounted policeman?"

A faint tinge of recognition as I squint at him. "Who are you?"

"You know me, Grace, don't you remember? Doesn't this park remind you of someplace?"

I reach my thoughts back into the snowy past.

"Vaguely. This looks like Abel's Place. Were you there?"

"Was I there? Was I there?" he laughs good-naturedly. "Hell's bells, I built the place, that's all!"

No mistaking the colorful language.

"Abel McGregor!" I shake my head in disbelief. "But you, you, well, you look so different! Last I recall, you were zooming around on that yellow scooter."

"Traded it in for Pegasus here. Dropped a few pounds and healed my hips, too, in case you can't tell." A cloud of dust escapes as he slaps his jeans.

I look him up and down. "You look good, Abel, as hardy as when you married Camelia, but why are you dressed like that guy on TV...what was his name?"

"Don't recall. I always like the idea, though, maybe from Aurora's silly fantasy about me rescuing her from that bobcat while on Pegasus, and it gives me an identity when I visit places.

Course, the kids don't always know about him, but that's OK, they know about cowboys." He flashes a flirty grin. "You're looking pretty snazzy yourself, Grace."

I feel my face grow hot, and wonder how I never noticed that his eyes are such a cornflower blue. "Thanks. So what are you doing here?"

He shrugs. "Well, I've been keeping kind of an eye on you, figuring you might need some help from time to time, like I did when I was new at this. And the Crossover can be tricky. Anyway, the amusement park is for me what your kitchen is for you."

"The last I heard of you, the state took the park under that eminent domain law for a new highway, then Camelia took off to Reno and filed for divorce."

He looks down and kicks the dirt.

"Oh, I'm sorry, that just slipped out. It was her fault as much as yours. She really could be such a priss."

He shakes his head, laughs again, and I find myself laughing along with him.

"My sister could starch a shirt with a lift of her eyebrow. I remember one time when we were kids she set up a picnic along the creek, all fancy with a checkered tablecloth and nice little basket, and she had her parasol opened so as not to get sun on her 'lily white' skin, and we decided to stage an Indian raid. We dressed up in some of Mama's old rags, painted our faces with beet juice and flour, and went whooping over to her picnic.

"You should've seen her jump up, screaming like to raise the dead, and dash off with her petticoats in a panic. She took off running while looking backwards, and ran right off the ledge and fell into the creek, the one that was full of crawdaddies! I never laughed so hard in all my life."

Abel guffaws at the mental picture of his fastidious wife as a young girl, with her parasol and fancy hat, swimming with the crawdads in the scummy creek.

"I swear she waged revenge on us a hundred different ways for the rest of that summer, but it was still worth it."

"Yeah, she was an easy mark for teasing, because she got so upset. But I suppose I overdid it, too, through the years."

I shoot him a glance and he grins again. "You're right. I'm not really that sorry."

There it is, his ornery look. I really had forgotten what a charmer he was in his youth. He grew so huge and gruff as he got older.

"You don't need to be sorry. You gave her a nice home, children, plenty of money in the bank, all the clothes and jewelry she wanted, she really had nothing to complain about. OK, I'll go along with the western theme today."

I pull some dough from my pocket, and sing up a fringed

white suede dress and red cowboy boots, then bring forth a jet black mare with a white diamond on her forehead. Turning to mount my horse, I invite Abel to join me for a walk.

"Sure. But first I have something to show you. It might be kind of upsetting, so feel free to just take a peek, and if you like, we'll leave right then. So we'll bring the horses, OK?"

I nod, curious. He takes both horses' reins in one hand and my arm in the other, and we move around the park, through the baseball field and into the grassy meadow where I woke up.

Seated on a fallen log with our horses grazing nearby, Abel and I peer through the mists. A crowd of nearly one hundred people are gathered at a funeral.

"It's tough, Gracie, watching a funeral," Abel said. "It could always be for someone you know."

I shade my eyes with my hand to get a closer look. "Huh. Some of those folks do look familiar." As I look more closely through the wisps of clouds and focus hard, I think I recognize many of the people in the crowd.

Sure enough! There are my sons and their families, Lily and Iris and my great granddaughter Poppy, my niece and nephew and grand niece Aurora together with her family, Abel's sister Inez and her kids, Ginny and my goddaughter, Abby, and many of my neighbors and former Sunday School students, including Connie.

"How strange! I do know a lot of those folks. And you know some of them, too."

"Really? Like who?"

"Well, for starters, there's my daughter, Lily. She's getting ready to retire from teaching, you know. But I have a feeling she'll continue to teach part time, or maybe substitute. You don't just walk away from your life's calling after 30 years.

"And her husband, Mitch, you only saw him now and then, do you remember? He is a wonderful man, has the patience of Job. Works for the Savings and Loan. They're planning to renew their wedding vows in Cancun next year for their anniversary.

"And my granddaughter, Iris, she's got her doctorate now – first one in the family! Looks like her two best friends are there with her, Laura and Cassidy. They're all going to be Psychologists. But you'd recall Iris as the indignant princess arguing with Aurora over who would be The Boss at The Shack."

He laughs. "Sorry, but Iris didn't stand a chance."

I join in. "Right, well, Her True Majesty is down there, too, in case you don't recognize her."

"Oh, I've kept up with Aurora and all her doings," he looks wistful. "Always regretted that I didn't get to attend her high school graduation, or college, either, or hold her little ones." He sighs. "Who else do you see?"

"Well, that little one with the head of curly, dark hair is

my great granddaughter, Poppy."

"Grace, she looks so much like you!"

"I hear that a lot, when people see photographs of me when I was younger. I think she also has some resemblance to Hiram, though."

"You're just saying that to be loyal. You don't need to do that anymore. Truth is, I always thought Hiram took you for granted."

I ignore him, and continue. "Oh, there's your sister, Inez! And Mona, did you know she's planning to become a mounted police officer?"

He nods, smiling. "I did know that, and Cecil's there, too. He's in high school now, just landed a summer job at the new Home Depot in Lamont. The manager is his basketball coach, and already likes him."

"He always was a responsible kid."

"Too much so, maybe. Anyway, he plans to marry a little neighbor girl, Shelley. One of those lucky couples who will be lifelong sweethearts, I imagine. They had an auspicious beginning: she threw up on him, and then they started reading the Song of Solomon together. You can imagine where that went..."

"No fooling? How did they find it?"

"In a box of stored books. Course, I might've helped them along a bit. Never hurts to give romance a nudge, right, Grace? Anyway, let's just say I've been keeping an eye on those kids, sometimes they need bailing out of trouble, especially Mona. How do you know so much about them?"

"From the letters that Lily read to me over the years, it really helped me stay up with the news. You wouldn't believe how many people kept writing to us, it helped so much."

"People usually like to help, if we let them know how. Who's the tall blonde in the flight attendant uniform?"

"That's Abby, the one in trouble with that abusive husband when I got stuck in her thoughts, and you saved her and shook me out of there. Her mother Ginny's there, too."

"Right, I hadn't realized it was her, I just knew you were in trouble. And, I wanted to tell you, Grace," he looks away, embarrassed. "I'm really sorry about what all happened to you at those nursing homes."

I swallow hard. "You know about all of that?"

"I'm just glad you're out of there."

"Me, too! Anyway, now Abby flies out of Seattle, she stood down her ex-husband one more time before he finally decided to leave her alone, and she's been dating again. Her karate instructor fell head over heels for her."

"I can see why. She's a knockout! Looks like Princess Grace."

"I always thought so, too."

He squints harder. "Does that lady on the right have scoliosis?"

"Ah, no, she's a former Sunday School student of mine. Her back was injured by a drunk driver when she was in high school. She's a physical therapist and also teaches yoga; says it really helps her. But it took a crippled patient of hers to heal her spirit. She was pretty bitter."

"Sergeant Reyes."

"Don't tell me you know Ben!"

"He put up a little cottage over near Half Dome, likes to rock climb. Plays a mean game of poker, too. And he said we're invited over to visit when things settle down."

I shake my head, smiling. *Don't know why anything here surprises me anymore.* "OK Well, about Connie, she's working at the V.A. Hospital now. People just adore her. I'd like to see her find someone, but I have a feeling she's going to take romance very slowly. She's cautious in life."

"Probably due to her history."

I nod in agreement. "Probably so." Then I lean down and cup my ear. "The preacher is starting to talk."

"Known far and wide for her generous volunteering of time and energy, her sweet nature, and her mouth watering apple pies! Is there anyone here who would like to speak about Grace before we surrender her to her final resting place?"

I gasp, and turn sharply to Abel, tears welling up. "Oh my Lord! Is that my funeral? Did I finally die?"

His face crinkles as he smiles sadly at me and puts his arm around my shoulders, "Well, they don't usually have funerals for the living. I'm sorry, Gracie, I know it's hard to take in. It's OK to have a good cry, if you like."

His arm smells like leather and hay. I quickly wipe my eyes and sniffle. "I feel like I've already done more crying than I had tears for. How long have I been dead?"

He hesitates. "That kind of depends on how you think about it, Grace. Your brain has been dead for a long while now, you just had trouble making up your mind about whether to live there or here. But time isn't such an issue here, you know, not nearly so important as in that other life."

"Man, it really ticks me off that after a lifetime of wondering about what death might be like, I died and can't remember anything about it! I was in a dream, at my homestead, and I baked up a whole world from my kitchen, and it was beautiful and magical, but there was this maddening well with silvery water that never reflected anything. I could hear people's voices and sometimes even their thoughts coming from somewhere under the water, it seemed like. It was the craziest thing!

"And I got so frustrated because I kept trying to help people, but they couldn't hear me, and I couldn't reach them, no matter what I did."

"Seems like you did help them, after all, by all the things you taught them when you were healthy," he says, in a low, gravelly voice that gives me little shivers. "But just so you know, now that you're truly here, you'll find it's easier to make appearances over there, when you really need to."

"I hope so."

"A well, huh? That's interesting. For me it was a tun-
nel. I'm claustrophobic, you know. And you can't swim,
can you?"

I shake my head.

"Was there a well on your property back home?"

"No, that's the thing. Only here, in Possibilities. That's
what I called my dream world. Say!" I sit upright. "I'm still
in my dream world! And you're here, too, aren't you?"

He chews thoughtfully on a stalk of grass. "I am indeed.
So then what happened in your old world?"

"Well, I could hear my kids debating about whether or
not to let my body die. I was being kept alive with a feeding
and drinking tube in my stomach, for a long time, I guess."
It's so degrading to say it all out loud.

He looks out toward the horizon as if to give me space.
"That was a hard as nails situation, for you and for them.
They hated seeing you like that."

I nod. "They did, and who can blame them? If I had
been standing over one of their beds for years, waiting for
a sign that never came, I'd be wondering, too, what is the
right thing."

Abel leans back and studies the clouds. "So you heard
the kids talking about it all, then what happened?"

"Well, I figured if they let my body die, then I would
lose all of Possibilities, all of this," I sweep my hand
across the landscape, "and more, all of everything. So I
worked up my courage; I did tell you that I don't know

how to swim, right? Oh yes, and I heard your voice! You suggested the rope."

He turns to smile at me.

"Well, anyhow, I gotta say, I've had lots of new and different experiences in Possibilities, but jumping into that well was the scariest thing I ever did, because I did it as me, not as someone else."

"That was brave of you, sure enough. I don't know if I would've had the nerve to jump into a well like that one, even though I do know how to swim."

I study the horizon and murmur, "So I died, but Possibilities didn't die, after all. So I was wrong about that all along."

He looks at me intently. "Now isn't that just the silliest idea I ever heard? That all of your creation would stop just because your body wore out? This is your new world, you just didn't know it. It seems to me that you're here, Grace, and you're supposed to be here, and this is a real place, and that's that."

"And where do you suppose 'here' really is, Abel?"

He sighs. "I've given that a lot of thought. Here's my idea about it. You know how you were able to dissolve into your folks' thoughts, I think you compared it to being in the spaces of a honeycomb, right?"

I nod.

"Well, maybe we've had it all wrong, the notion that eternity is 'out there.' Maybe eternity is 'in there,' in the spaces between things. Kind of like how the spaces in between the walls of your house don't look like anything, but those spaces form the rooms you exist in, the backdrop for life, the essential soup you 'swim' in. Like a zero is nothing, but it holds a place, and that helps to make the number, and give it meaning.

"What if this place is 'in between' others, maybe even smaller, or tucked in, kind of?"

I can't help but smile. "Gee, you've become quite the philosopher. I never knew you had the interest."

He laughs. "Oh, I had the interest, just never had the time! And I can't say that I have all the answers, I've just been trying to engage in more flexible thinking since I got here. The old ways of thinking just don't seem ample enough."

Tentatively, afraid to believe that it might be true for fear it will all vanish, I look around. Nothing has changed. I'm still young. Possibilities is still abundant and thriving. It all seems to be OK. "And here I thought it was just a dream."

Abel stands up and stretches. "Best damn dream I ever had, if it is," he smiles. "Maybe that other was a nightmare! Maybe we just woke up."

"But I thought I would see Jesus or the Virgin Mary or at least St. Peter. Hope I haven't gone the wrong direction."

"Beats me. I haven't seen them, either. But then, I haven't called on them. Something tells me that if you want to see them, you can, you just have to ask. Anyway, as best I can figure, this is our everlasting, or maybe just a step on the path to our everlasting. Either way, I'm glad I get to share it with you."

He smiles again and waits quietly as I gaze down through the violet dusk at my funeral gathering. A rhythmic symphony arises from the crickets in the fields nearby. Off in the distance, a yellow biplane is doing loop-de-loops.

"Let's go," I stand up myself and sweep the dried grass from my dress. "They're pretty much finished."

The bittersweet intensity has drained me. It's so hard when things end. I've come a long way from my first day of discovery in Possibilities. Created a community, dissolved into countless identities and thoughts and experienced new places and events, agonized over my inability to reach my family and to wake up, and lost my beloved companion, Eureka.

"Are you OK, Gracie?"

"I just miss them all so much. Even though I can hold them in my mind, it's different than holding them in my arms. Dying means saying Goodbye to the time and place we shared, and the way we shared it. That won't ever be quite the same again."

"Are you homesick?"

"Maybe. Not so much longing for a place, more like longing for a time when people and events come together just so, in a way they never will again. Maybe it's more like 'timesickness.'"

"Well, don't forget, you left part of yourself with them, too. Kind of like we leave a trail of personal breadcrumbs through the times we live."

I look back at the funeral once more, then climb on my horse and trot toward the orange and pink clouds of sunset. Abel tips his hat to the crowd below and turns Pegasus around to follow me.

We ride quietly together through meadows and woods, until I pull up in amazement.

"I don't believe it! Look!"

Abel reins in his horse and turns his gaze to where I'm pointing.

Across the creek, partially hidden by the lazy branches of a weeping willow tree, stand the wooden arch, sideposts and stone walls of an old well.

"Well, I'll be. Never noticed that before. Do you want to go investigate?"

The glade surrounding the well looks so inviting. Dappled sunlight, ripples of cool water flowing past, birds chirping in the trees. So tempting. Abel's blue eyes are twinkling, promising adventure and fun.

"No, I think we can save it for another day."

"Fair enough."

We continue, and before long I hear him humming an old song, one I recognize. "Isn't that from Cole Porter?"

He nodded, smiling. As I recall, you really like to

dance, Grace."

"I do! Say, did you ever dance the Beguine?"

He begins swaying his upper body to keep time. "Sure I did, tons of times! I was quite the hoofer in my day, you know. Say! Wanna try out Fred Astaire and Eleanor Powell?"

"OK, but I get the first turn at being Fred."

Back in Iowa, my family puts my body to rest as they wrap their memories of me in love, the best conduit of all, for safekeeping.

So now I am everything I was, and so much more. This feels so right, so natural, that I wonder why I never thought of my life in these terms before.

Meanwhile, Abel and I continue with this new chapter, new friends, and new endeavors. We help out when we can, and try to teach all our people to use their gifts, to not forget their lineage.

Creators, and created, all of us, and all of you, in a world called Possibilities.

With Love,

Grace and Abel.

Author Biography

Colleen Golden writes fiction for adults and young adults under her nom de plume, and also publishes nonfiction in the field of neuropsychology. She was born in the Midwest, raised on the West Coast, and resides in Colorado with her husband of 25 years, where she has a successful career in psychology and library/information science. She is an avid practitioner of yoga, loves hiking, biking, and any beach with a palm tree, pina coladas and a really absorbing book in hand.

Book Club Questions

1. Did Grace remind you of anyone you know? In what way?

2. How did Grace's voice and viewpoints change through the course of the story?

3. Did you feel that her family made the right decision(s) along the course of her hospitalization? What might you have done differently?

4. Abel weaves his way in and out of the story, becoming more important over time. What role did you feel he played in Grace's life and afterlife?

5. Grace is bemused, then perplexed and ultimately enraged by The Well. Yet it proved to be her point of crossing. Do you think she suspected this all along?

6. Each chapter features an important person in Grace's life. Do you think that we all have the opportunity to somehow interact with our loved ones even while in coma? After death?

CPSIA information can be obtained at www.ICGtesting.com
Printed in the USA
LVOW11s0416150114

369418LV00001B/20/P